D1522666

Chloe

JERRY LEPPART

CHLOE

iUniverse books may be ordered through booksellers or by contacting:

iUniverse
1663 Liberty Drive
Bloomington, IN 47403
www.iuniverse.com
1-800-Authors (1-800-288-4677)

Because of the dynamic nature of the internet, any web addresses or links contained in this book may have changed since publication and may no longer be valid. The views expressed in this work are solely those of the author and do not necessarily reflect the views of the publisher, and the publisher hereby disclaims any responsibility for them.

This is a work of fiction. All the characters, names, incidents, organizations, and dialogue in this novel are either the products of the author's imagination or are used fictitiously.

Any people depicted in stock imagery provided by Getty Images are models, and such images are being used for illustrative purposes only. Certain stock imagery © Getty Images.

ISBN: 978-1-5320-6202-5 (sc)
ISBN: 978-1-5320-6204-9 (hc)
ISBN: 978-1-5320-6203-2 (e)

Library of Congress Control Number: 2018914291

Print information available on the last page.

iUniverse rev. date: 01/12/2019

Chapter 1

A man looks at something and sees what it
is. A wise man sees what it may become.
                              —Billy Two Bears

MY MOTHER WAS DEAD AT MY BIRTH. ACTUALLY, SHE DIED
nine months before I was born. My name is Chloe, and
I am a clone.

I am at my father's funeral. I am with my friends. I
have not told them. I do not know how to tell them. How
do you tell them that you are not … that you are …

Human cloning is illegal. I don't know whether it is
against the law or against moral judgment. But I am
here. And I am truly an illegal alien. Not much is known
about the results of cloning. They have cloned sheep. And
the sheep was the exact duplication of the donor. The
DNA is the same. But they have found that, while it is the
same, the cloning process shaves a little off the original
chromosomes. I may look like my mother. I may be an
exact duplicate of my mother. But I am a little different.
I have a shelf life shorter than normal.

I went to the clinic that, well, made me. They were
quite tight-lipped about it. A lot of "If we did this" and
"If you are that." It is still illegal, and I could see their
point. But they did give me some information—saying

it was relevant if I was who I said I was, if someone had made me what I am. Nothing is known for sure, because they have only dealt with animals—or so they say. Dolly, the sheep clone, was a true sheep, but she had some problems and did not live a full sheep's life. Could be just her, but it could be something else. As I said before, a clone has the same DNA and same chromosomes, but something is shaved off. It's like why cousins shouldn't marry. Their offspring will have DNA and chromosomes, but they are different. The people at the clinic said that they couldn't be certain but that someone like me, if I was what I said I was, might have some problems with stress. And they advised against my having children, as that would have the biggest stress on my body and—well, it would be just better if I adopted. But I've always wanted to be a mother, ever since I was a child playing house with dolls, thinking about when I would grow up and have a husband and a house and children. Someone, somewhere, gave me life, and every breath I take is extra credit. I want a daughter. To go through life not having children simply by believing that I couldn't or shouldn't, when in reality I could have and should have, would be tragic. I want to give life to someone. I want to extend myself. And if something does happen, hell, I've reached the bonus round anyway. So I'm going to live my life as I should, not in fear of what might be but in glorious hopefulness of what can be.

Chapter 2

Three Days Before

"I'm here to see Dr. Ahmann," I say.

The receptionist looks at me quizzically. "Do you have an appointment?"

"No," I say. "Tell him that I am Chloe Murphy and I am here to talk to him about an operation … a procedure twenty-two years ago."

"Well, the doctor is very busy," says the receptionist. "He has a full schedule …"

"Please tell him that Chloe Murphy is here to see him. And I'll wait."

The receptionist stares for a moment, and then she gets up and disappears around the corner. I go over to a chair and pick up a magazine. I flip the pages without sitting down.

"Ms. Murphy?"

I turn around. A man of about forty-five stands by the reception desk. At six feet, with jet-black hair combed back, he could have walked out of *GQ* magazine. Gray trousers on top of highly polished oxfords, a white smock with "Mark Ahmann" embroidered above his left breast pocket. "Yes," I say. "I'm Chloe Murphy, and I need about ten minutes of your time. I'm sorry I don't have an appointment, but it's very important to me. And I suspect it will be quite important to you."

Dr. Ahmann looks me over for a moment. I can see a glint of admiration in his eyes, almost an appreciation. "Yes," he says. "I know who you are."

I look at him, somewhat puzzled. "You know who I am?"

He turns to the receptionist. "Would you put my appointments back about fifteen minutes or so?"

The receptionist nods and turns to her computer.

"I think we should talk in private," says Dr. Ahmann, motioning me to an open room. We enter, and he closes the door behind me.

"Chloe," says Dr. Ahmann, "I was going to contact you, but I thought I should wait until after the funeral. But I'm glad you came in. You may not know this, but I have been following your progress from afar since you were born. Actually, before you were born. I want to tell you everything. You deserve to hear the whole truth."

"Good," I say. "That is why I'm here."

"Let's start at the beginning," says Dr. Ahmann. "This, as you know, is an in vitro clinic. We take in women who cannot get pregnant and help them. *In vitro* comes from Latin, meaning 'in glass.' The common term is 'test tube babies,' but this is a little misleading because we use dishes rather than test tubes—but that's a small point. This is how it works. When a woman cannot get pregnant in the usual manner, we take an egg, or eggs, from her body and mix it with sperm from the father-to-be, and then, if and when fertilization takes place, we implant the fertilized eggs back into the patient. With any luck, a viable fetus will form and pregnancy occurs.

"Cloning is very similar. I'm going to get a little technical here, but bear with me. There are two types of cells within the human body: germ cells and somatic cells. Germ cells are the cells of sperm and egg. All the other cells are somatic cells. The difference is that the germ cells have

4

only one set of chromosomes. When they combine, there will be two sets of chromosomes within the cell, each set contributing some hereditary trait of each participant—I mean, the male and the female. But in cloning, we want to transfer the entire set of chromosomes from the donor to the new entity. To do this, we take an egg and remove the nucleus. Then we place a somatic cell with both sets of chromosomes into the egg and then implant the egg inside the surrogate. This way, we have a complete duplicate of the original donor.

"When your father came to me, he explained that his wife had been critically injured in a car accident and was not going to live. He loved your mother very much and said he didn't know if he could go on without her. This was twenty-two years ago, in 1997. Dolly, the sheep, had been successfully cloned, and there was a lot of excitement in the air. A lot of cloning of plants and bacteria and insects, but this was a large mammal. Human cloning was a real possibility. There were a lot of questions, ethically, morally, about this, but after considerable thought, I agreed to try the procedure. Nine months later, you were born."

"But why didn't you or Dad tell me?"

"We did not tell you, to protect you. The formative years are very difficult, and the teenage years, as you may know, can be very trying on anyone who is not 'normal.' Can you imagine the teasing and bullying you would have received if everyone knew what you were? You would have been called a freak or worse. There's a lyric in the song by the Police, 'Don't Stand So Close to Me,' remember ... 'You know how bad girls get!' It's true. I have a daughter, and I would not want her scoffed at and ridiculed. So your father and I decided to wait to tell you about yourself until later, until you could handle it. I guess that time is now."

"I can appreciate that, and thank you. But it must have been hard for you to not get credit for your work. I mean, you could have been famous. You could have been like—what's his name?—Dr. Barnard."

"Yes, I could have been famous. But the chances are I would have been more infamous. Dr. Christiaan Barnard was the first doctor to successfully transplant a human heart. But that was, and still is, considered a lifesaving operation. What I did was a life-giving procedure. There are all kinds of ethical, moral, and, not the least to say, theological questions. Ian Wilmut and Keith Campbell at the Roslin Institute in Edinburgh, Scotland, cloned Dolly the sheep. They received plaudits, and they received derision for their efforts. Many people believe that this is playing God. And perhaps in a certain sense it is. I am Catholic, and although I did what I thought was right, bringing a new life into the world, the Catholic Church has other views. Excommunication was and is a real possibility. You can disagree with the church, but you can't let them know you disagree. So I am satisfied with what I did, and that is enough for me."

"Yes, I can see that. But can you tell me a little more about me? The main one is, What are my prospects—I mean, how long will I live?"

"That's a tough one. Dolly was a healthy sheep. But she only lived for six years, only half the life expectancy of sheep. Which is another reason your father and I did not want to publicize this. They don't really know how she died. Although she had lung cancer, there may have been other factors contributing to the development of the cancer. Some speculate that she was born with a genetic age of six years, the same age as the donor sheep. Another thought is that they found that she was born with short telomeres, which contributed to an advanced aging process. It was as if the cloning process had provided an exact duplicate body, but something, somehow had been shaved off. And we don't know why. It was as if all the parts were there, but something was changed. I mean, the parts were the right size and contained the right matter, but it was as if she was a shadow or something. I can just put it as something was different. And that's when I stopped any further procedures. It was as if we were playing God and, as it turns out, not playing him well." He shook his head. "To this day, we don't know what went wrong. It seemed so perfect. But it just went wrong. I guess there are some things in nature that we are just better off leaving alone."

"What about me, Doctor?" I ask. "Have I had some shaving off?"

The doctor shook his head again. "I don't know," he said. "It was never done on humans before, so I don't know what to tell you."

"Doctor," I say, "I didn't come here to have you tell me that you don't know. I want to know what you think."

"There's no way of knowing," says the doctor. "Humans are not sheep. Perhaps you will live a long life." He shrugged. "But as a precaution, take it easy. Don't stress yourself too much. That is all I can suggest."

I stare at him for a long moment. "Is that it?" I ask.

He shrugs again.

I take a deep breath. "Well, thank you for your time, Doctor," I say, stand up, and turn for the door.

"Ah," says Dr. Ahmann. "There is one thing."

I turn back to him.

"You might think about not having children. That might be more stress than your body can handle."

I close my eyes and bring my right hand to my forehead.

"But then again," says the doctor, "we just don't know."

Chapter 3

I AM AT THE FUNERAL OF MY FATHER. AM I MY MOTHER? I have the same biology. I see pictures of her. I see her smile. I have the same teeth and the same lips. But when I see pictures of her, her smile, she seems to light up the room. You can see people gravitate toward her. They want to be around her. You can see it in the pictures. I wish I had known her. She was the kind of woman who would make a man go outside the laws of nature to keep her. Am I that kind of woman? Would someone care for me enough to not want to go on without me? I have friends. I have a boyfriend. He is sitting next to me. But there is no way that he loves me that way. To be sure, my mother and father had a long life together, but jeez, could I ever find someone to do that? Could I ever be worthy of that kind of devotion? I knew my father. He was a great man in my eyes. I wish I had some of him in me. I wish I was really his daughter. Then I would be sharing his chromosomes. And I could be like him. But I am me, Chloe. And I am my mother, Jenny. And I don't know how to act. You can call me, and I will come. But I will not be the person you called. I will be part of that person and part of something else. I have to find who I am. I have to find what I am. I've got to find me.

I'm sitting in a pew, looking at the picture of my father on the altar. He wasn't much of a churchgoer. In fact, he didn't really like religion. But he had to have a funeral somewhere. When we asked him where he would like it, he would say that it didn't matter to him. He would be dead. He said that it only matters to the survivors. And if they feel more comfortable in a church, what the hell ... oops.

My sister Lisa is at the lectern fighting back tears. She is really a strong woman. She is telling stories of Dad. She is really my half sister, or at least, that is what she was before I found out my situation. I still consider her my half sister. And changing the relationship I have with my siblings does not make much sense with all the things that are twirling around in my head. My dad and Lisa's mom got married young. Only nineteen. Lisa was born soon after. Two and a half years later, my other half sister, Andrea, was born. My father always said it was youthful pride that ended the marriage after some seven years or so. They were just kids, not much older than I am now. I can't imagine the stress of raising a family while working your way through college. It wasn't any one thing—no hard moment, no adultery, no drunken brawls. It's just that, once you go down a certain path, youthful pride takes over, and you are just stepping aside, watching the world turn your life upside down.

Well, it happened. There was some time apart. Dad didn't talk too much about that. He just said it was the low time in his life. I imagine it was really difficult figuring out who he was, going from a father and husband to a distant father and divorcé. Not that much different from what I am feeling now. A change in your life's image that you could never have seen coming. He always said he was sad that he couldn't be a better father to his first two kids. It was tough, but he tried. He said that he was fortunate enough after a while—he had a good relationship with his ex, and when she got a chance to move to California, he was excited to have the girls come and live with him. Holy shit! Two teenage girls, sixteen and thirteen, coming to live with a bachelor while possibly harboring resentment at their mother abandoning them. There's a hand to draw to.

A couple of years later, when he was at the end of that roller coaster ride, he met my mother, Jenny. The timing was right, and they were married within eighteen months. By that time, Lisa had moved out and had found a boyfriend. Andrea was still living with my father and his wife. What a mix. The fur was flying. I think Andi's rebellion was just a reflex of a feeling of abandonment. It was not meant to be by her mother, and it certainly was not meant to be by her father. He desperately wanted to be a good father, and here was his chance. But there were tides pulling against her that she did not understand, and perhaps her independence was a shield. She never wanted to be dependent on anyone again. Perhaps it was the same abandonment that my father felt when his mom left him. He certainly messed up a lot when that happened. It took time, but he pulled himself through. But Andi still has a shield around her. If she doesn't get close to anyone, she can't get hurt. She has a boyfriend; she calls him a male companion. My father really liked him. (He liked Monty Python, case closed.) Maybe enough time has passed to where she can let herself be loved again.

My brother, Jeffrey, was born within two years, followed by my sister, Elizabeth, two years hence. My father always said that Jeff was the best person he had ever met, after my mother, of course. And it's true. Even now, I haven't met anyone as cheerful and loving and willing to help as my brother, Jeff. I have to share his genes somewhere in the mix. But what am I? Am I his sister or a continuation of his mother? It's so damned confusing.

And then there is Elizabeth. She is my sister; she is my daughter; my sister; my daughter. I feel like I'm in Chinatown. Somebody slap me, will ya?

Elizabeth is kind and caring and beautiful. When she walks into a bar, all the male heads turn and watch her as she glides across the floor. They can't help it, any more than I can stop my pupils expanding when I see a hunk of a guy. Fortunately, she is shy enough that it does not go to her head. If anything, she is self-conscious about her beauty and would never think of using it to her advantage.

And what should I think about my father? He gave me life. But should I hate him for what he did? Or should I love him for what he did? Should I take him at his word—that he loved my mother so much that he couldn't bear to be without her? Does he love me, or am I just a memory? Does that make me a trinket, a bauble that he could be with to think of someone else? Or should I just be thankful that he gave me life with all of its confusion? I don't know how to feel. Would it be better if he had not told me? I could have a normal life. God, that's all I want—a normal life. I don't want to be a freak. For Christ's sake, I'm not even a freak of nature. There is nothing natural about me. I'm man-made. I'm just a freak. But as I pause, I realize that I am here because someone loved someone. And I think that before I can understand myself, I must get to understand that other someone—my mother.

Joe takes my hand and gives it a gentle squeeze. He is sitting next to Elizabeth and her husband. We kids have decided to sit in the first pew on the left in a descending order by age. So Lisa and her husband have the seats closest to the aisle, followed by Andi and her domestic partner, Jeff and his wife, Elizabeth and her husband, and Joe and me. I suppose that's best. You have to have some order. I always thought I was closest to our father, who art in heaven (I hope). Since I was unencumbered with siblings growing up, I thought I had his undivided attention. But he always made a point of keeping in touch with all of his children. I'm sure he loved us all. But I still feel that there was something special. Considering my situation, there was nothing odd. Nothing weird. No feelings that should not have been there. I think he just wanted me to grow up and to be with me while I did. Maybe it was just a presence that he wanted. Not a picture in an album. But a real person. He was with me when I needed him to be there and left me as much room as I needed when I needed it. I remember the father-daughter dance. I think it was third grade. I was quite shy, but my best friend, who lived across the street, wanted to go to the dance, and so we had to tag along. It was a dance where all the girls would wear poodle skirts. So I had my poodle skirt on but was too shy to go out on the dance floor. My friend was very gregarious, and she and her dad were all over the dance floor. After we had our picture taken, my father coaxed me out on the floor. I was pretty small, so a traditional clutching was out of the picture. My father took my hands in his and told me to stand on his shoes. I looked over at my friend and her dad and, sure enough, they were dancing toe on toe. I put my feet on my father's shoes, and we sashayed around the dance floor. Looking back, I think that was when I started to get over my shyness. I was like everyone else. I could do it.

Later, on my first date, my boyfriend came to the door.

My father let him in, and when I appeared at the top of the stairs, I could almost see his chest expand. It was a day that he said he had been waiting for. His little girl was now grown up. Of course, when my boyfriend led me out the door, it was followed by a reminder of what time to be home, followed by "Daaaad!"

Although he had coached my brother and sister in baseball and basketball, I found my way into soccer. I was pretty good at it, and my father was at every game.

I dated in high school, but never seriously. Maybe Dad was too close to me. I don't think so. I think I just wasn't interested enough in anyone to get serious, like some of my friends who went gaga over the next guy filling out jeans. But it was in college at the University of Minnesota that I met Joe Thomas. He was a couple of years older than me. I didn't believe in love at first sight, but there was something about him that caught my eye. It was at a frat party. He got a little drunk, and I had to drive him home. His wallet fell out as he lay against the seat, and when I let him out in his driveway, I somehow forgot to give it to him. I got out and helped him to his door. He said goodbye with a hug and a belch. Nice intro.

The next day, I drove over to his place and gave him his wallet back. He apologized for the previous night but asked me out. Well, of all the nerve! Of course, I was coy when I accepted. We've been together ever since. We are sort of engaged to be engaged.

Lisa, Andi, and Jeff have given eulogies, reminders of their memories of our father. Elizabeth is too broken up to participate. Some other friends have spoken kind memories, and we are coming to the end. Fortunately, my father had time to plan his funeral. If you can call this planning. He did not want any pastor or priest giving a sermon. He did not want anyone who did not know him talking over his grave. Only people who knew him and cared for him should have the last words. Only one picture of him was to be on the altar. He talked about the music he wanted played in his memory. We had to talk him out of ACDC's "Highway to Hell." He liked the song, but we thought it totally inappropriate. For once in our lives, we held sway. He always thought Paul Simon's "The Boxer" was the best song ever. But once again, this was a funeral. Not appropriate. REO Speedwagon's "Rolling with the Changes" and Metallica's "One"? Not so much. So we ended up with his favorite, Schubert's "Ave Maria," with Michael Bublé to open the affair. And after everyone has said their piece, but with everyone still in their seats, we'll rock them out with Chicago's "I'm a Man." We tried to talk him out of it, but he said he wanted them bouncing in their pews.

When the music starts, I look around when the bass, drums, and sticks start clacking and, sure enough, there are some suits and dresses moving to the beat. If the man is looking down right now, he's got to be smiling.

When the music ends, Lisa gets up from the pew and tells the audience that we will meet them at the country club for lunch and remembrances, but that we will be a few minutes late. Then she ushers out the children, their spouses and significant others, children and grandchildren to make a circle before the altar. She tells us to bow our heads and send Dad off with our thoughts and our prayers. As we bow our heads in silence, I steal a glance at the picture of our father. He is smiling. I've seen the picture before. But it is as if this is the first time I have seen it.

He is smiling, and I am comforted by his memory and saddened for his departure. I know that they all have a sense of loss. But he raised me by himself. And I had him to myself. No sharing of his affection. Or at least, that is how he made me feel. I know he loved all of his kids and each had a special place in his heart. But I felt special. Although he did not share the faith of any religion, he did not dismiss it either. And I have not prayed to a god for years. But now I bow my head and let my eyelids squeeze out the tears as I ask for heavenly grace to find a place for this fallen angel.

We are at the country club for the after-funeral luncheon. We have had the receiving line, and now everyone is seated at an appropriate table. Lisa is with her husband and her three kids and one son-in-law. Andi is with her partner, Raha. Jeff is with his wife and two kids. Elizabeth, like Jeff, is married with two children. I am sitting with my boyfriend, Joe. He is a good man. But we really do not have a committed relationship. And I believe that we may be parting soon. I just feel that I have to be alone for a while. I may have to break up with Joe. It's really not fair to him. But it would be less fair if I could not give him what a committed relationship requires. He has no idea. I don't either. I just know that I have to do some things alone. And it may take a while. It may take a lifetime.

I'm kind of sad when I look around at my siblings. They are all quite happy in their relationships. No smoke on the horizon that I can see. I wish I could be like them, confident in who I am and what I am doing. And then it dawns on me. Lisa has herself, her husband, three kids, and a son-in-law. That's six. Andi has herself and Raha. That's two.

Jeff and Elizabeth have four apiece. *My god, they're all even. And I'm odd. Boy, am I ever odd.* I chuckle at the thought. If there was ever symbolism in my life, this is it. Poor Joe. I love him, and I feel for him because he doesn't see this coming. But I will do what I must do. There is a saying: "If you love something, let it go"—that's just bullshit. But I *will* have to let him go. I wish I could say it was noble. But it's not. It's selfish. There will be tears. And we will go our separate ways. And it will be done. And for me, it will only be the beginning.

Chapter 4

"DO YOU WANT ME TO COME IN?" ASKS JOE AS HE PULLS the car to the curb.

I shake my head. "No, Joe," I say.

"You sure?" he asks again. "I don't have any plans tonight. And I thought you might not want to be alone."

My heart sinks at the words. *Not be alone.* I have thought of the words, perhaps, but to hear them makes my heart sink. I know I must be alone. I know I have to get away. It's not that I want to be. It's that I have to be. And the thought of telling Joe is something I have dreaded. And now it is here. I can't let Joe go without telling him. I don't know if I will have the strength later. So now I have to break the heart of the person who I have loved more than anyone else. And I can't tell him the reason. He will ask, and he will not understand. But my journey, the journey that I must take, must begin now.

"Joe," I manage. "There is something that I have to tell you. I know that you will not understand. I'm not really sure that *I* understand it."

Joe looks confused. "Wha ... what is it?" he asks with a questioning look.

"Joe," I say. "I'm going to leave you."

Joe's lips curl up. "What the ...?"

"Joe," I continue. "There is something going on in my life. There is no other one, nothing like that. I still love you more than anyone. But something happened, and I have to get away. I know it's awful to leave you like this, and I hope you'll come to understand."

"I don't understand," says Joe. "I thought we were—"

"No," I say, putting my right index and middle fingers to his lips. "We were doing great. It's not that. And I know it's not fair not to tell you the reason. But it would be even worse if I left without telling you that I have to leave. Believe me—this is nothing about you. I still love you. And maybe I always will."

"Well, shit, lady," says Joe. "Where are you going?"

"That's just it," I say. "I don't know."

"What the hell?" says Joe.

"I just have to get away," I say. "Maybe I'll be back. I hope to be back. But I can't leave you without telling you. That would be cruel."

"So, that's it?" asks Joe.

I bring both hands to my cheeks as the tears start to overflow my eyelids. I can only nod.

Joe lets out a sigh. "Well, that's it," he says.

I swallow and wipe away the tears.

Joe puts his hand gently around the back of my neck. "Can I at least walk you to the door?"

I nod. We get out of the car, and Joe comes around to my side and takes my left hand in his. We don't talk as we cross the street to my father's house.

"I hope this isn't the last time I hold your hand," says Joe, forcing a smile.

I can't get the words out of my mouth. I only nod.

"I won't forget you," Joe says. "If you need me, you know where to find me."

He wipes away the tears from my cheek, only to have them reappear. He leans down and kisses me fully on the lips. He parts, walks slowly to his car, opens the door, and gets in without looking back at me. I hear the engine start and watch the love of my life disappear down the street.

I keep thinking about Lisa and Andi and Jeff and Elizabeth and how they are even and I am odd. Odd ... as John of Gaunt said, "Oh, how that term befits my composition." Am I a freak? Am I even human? I know that I have genes and chromosomes and whatever, but does that make me human? Are there others like me anywhere on this freaking planet? Can I reproduce? And if I could, what would they look like? What would they be?

Dr. Ahmann: "You want my educated opinion? Well, it's just a guess, but I would say that you could live a long life, or you could give birth. But in my estimation, you can't do both."

"But you gave me life, and my father gave me life, and my mother gave me life. All I want to do is to give life to someone as someone gave life to me."

"Well, genetically, the only purpose we have on earth is to give life. But that's just genetics speaking. We are adult humans, and we can make choices for ourselves."

"I want to have purpose to my life. I don't want to live my life as an abstraction, just a person with an asterisk after her name. I want my life to mean something. Not just for now. I want a continuation."

Chapter 5

I STOPPED BY MY GRANDPARENTS' HOUSE, JENNY'S PARENTS' house, on Garfield Avenue. No one was home, so I drove over to Richfield High School, where Jenny went to school. I'm trying to get a feel of something. I don't know. Just to see if there is something there. I tried to go in, but they have security now, and since I didn't have any business there, I had to turn around. So I'm standing in front of the school. It's a huge school. Bricks and mortar. It just seems so impersonal right now.

I know my mother was popular. At least, she had a lot of friends. Not that she was in the "in crowd." You've gotta be rich to be in the "in crowd" in high school. Or at least, your parents have to be rich. At least, that's what it was like when I went to high school. Oh, sure, the "innies" were nice to you. But you really couldn't be one of them. They had a clique, and there wasn't a glass ceiling, just glass walls. You'd see them blowing you a kiss from the passenger seat of their boyfriend's convertible as you stood on the corner waiting for the bus. I had friends. My mother had friends. But that was it. There's nothing here. Nothing I can feel. It's just a huge brick edifice. And that's all it is.

I drive back to the house on Garfield. There is a car

in the driveway now. I park my car, get out, and walk to the door.

"Hi," I say to the woman who opens the front door. "My name is Chloe. My grandparents lived in this house and raised my mother and uncle here."

"Uh-huh," says the woman.

"I was driving by, and I saw your car in the driveway," I say.

The woman nods somewhat questioningly.

"How long have you lived here?" I ask.

She looks up at the sky. "Oh, I don't know. Let me see. Twenty ... no, I'd say around twenty-five years."

"My grandparents were Rolf and Soli Hegel."

"Yes, I think that was their names."

"My mother died when I was very young. But my father tried to tell me everything about her. He told me about this house and Jenny, my mother, growing up here. I thought I might stop by, and if you don't mind—I know I'm asking a lot, but if you don't mind—I'd like to come in and look around."

"Oh," says the woman, somewhat taken aback. She looks out at my empty car and then at me. "Why, of course," she says. "I remember your grandparents, somewhat, now that you mention their names. Yes, please come in." She holds the door open wider.

I enter the house and smell something like bread baking in the kitchen. "You have done such a good job of keeping the house up," I say.

"Thank you," she says. "Charles does the outside, and I do the inside. We've been here a long time. And we both do our chores."

"My mother told me that she and her brother used to have to share a bedroom when they were young, and when Rolf and Soli had a party, they would sneak down to the upper landing and listen to the goings-on downstairs."

The woman smiles a bit.

"Would you mind if I went up and looked at the bedroom?"

"No, certainly you can go up and look. Follow me," she says and leads me up the stairs.

The two bedrooms are nondescript. What must be the master bedroom has a double bed and some clothing laid on the bed. The other bedroom is somewhat smaller but still has a double bed. It is crystal clean. No one has slept there in quite a while. I thank the lady and head down the stairs. I stop at the upper landing. I close my eyes and try to imagine two children huddled together, giggling at the gossip they hear from the adults down below. I smile to myself and head down the stairs. I turn into the living room. There is a couch against the far wall. My father had described how he and my mother were out to dinner. They were in a booth, and after they had finished dinner and poured the last glass of wine, he slid over to her side of the booth. He told her that he loved her with all of his heart and that he wanted to spend the rest of his life with her. And he asked her to marry him. He told me that my mother said that she would be proud to marry him. He presented a ring to her, and as he slid it on her finger, they kissed.

He told me that after the dinner, it seemed like they flew over to Rolf and Soli's house.

I stand before the empty couch. This is where my father and mother stood and asked for my mother's parents' blessing. I close my eyes. Shivers flow up my back to my shoulders and neck. My father reaches down and takes *my* hand. Rolf and Soli are sitting on the couch in front of us. Father tells them that he has asked for *my* hand in marriage and *I* have accepted. We are here to ask for their blessing. Rolf tries to remain stoic but manages, "Well, I 'spose that would be all right." Soli, with the excitement of a new bride herself, leaps off the couch and hugs *me*. Rolf rises and shakes my father's hand, welcoming him to the family. We switch, and Rolf hugs *me*, and Soli hugs my father.

"Do you remember anything?" asks the lady.

I open my eyes, and with a smile, I say "Yes." I turn to her and look straight into her eyes. "Yes, I do."

I pull into the driveway of our house. I still call it our house. It is the house I grew up in. I grew up here with my father. It was just the two of us. My brother and sister grew up in it before I was born. But since I was born, it has only been my father and me. And he was always there for me. He took me to the bus stop and waited with me until the bus came, waving to me as it pulled away. He would take me to the movies that I wanted to see. He would take me to practice for whatever sport I was into: soccer, basketball, softball. He was there to see me off on my first date. He insisted that the young man come into the house. I know my boyfriend was really nervous, but Dad held out his hand and gave him a firm handshake, not overpowering, but just firm and confident. They talked sports for a while as I was working at being late. When we left, he gave my boyfriend another handshake and told us to have a good time. When we got out to my boyfriend's car, my boyfriend said, "Your dad—he's cool." Oh my god, I was so proud I almost swallowed my tongue. How many teenage girls have their date tell them that their dad is "cool"? But he was. He made people feel at home. He wasn't overpowering, but genuinely interested in them. He was ... well ... "cool."

He taught me how to drive and provided a car. I could see a tear swelling in his eyes when I went off to college, and he helped me with my algebra when I really needed it. He was always there for me.

Did I feel something when I stood before that couch at Garfield? Yes, I'm sure I did. Was it actually my father's spirit that I felt? I don't know what it was. But there was definitely something. And what of the love that my father felt for me? Was it really for me? Did he love me for what and who I was, or was it just a remembrance of my mother? And as for me, am I Electra? Do I have an Electra complex? Do I love my father too much, or as Othello, "not wisely but too well"? All I know is that I can't stay in this house anymore. I've got to get away. I will try to find my mother, but I *have* to find myself.

Chapter 6

WE'RE PUTTING THE HOUSE ON THE MARKET. I AM STILL living there for now. But it is too big for me to maintain, and it's just right to sell it now and split up the equity. Lisa is handling it. She is the executor of the estate. She is very competent. I am very proud of my sister. Or my half sister. Or whatever. I am very proud of all of my "whatevers." They are all unique, but they are all great people. My father's genes must have had something to do with it, I guess.

I'm sorting through some items downstairs, looking for the three-man tent that my father used to take me camping in. I find it right next to our skis in a storage area. It's a three-man nylon tent, which is a little out of date with all the streamlined fold-over tents I see. But it was big and roomy and worked just fine for us. He showed me how to put up the tent, take it down, and pack it up. He showed me how to find wood. In campgrounds, the woods can be pretty well picked over by former campers. But he could always go a little deeper into the woods and come out with an armful. And he taught me how to build a fire, starting with pine needles, then twigs. Get the fire going and then comes the wood. Don't smother the fire by putting a lot of wood on right away. His motto was "One match, not paper." Using paper, to him, was like cheating. You might as well be staying at a KOA. He even showed me how to light a fire in the rain. Easy. Just bring along a candle and put it under the pine needles, and you can build a fire, even in the rain. Well, maybe a light mist.

I grab the tent and pull it out of the storage room. A ski gets knocked over as I pull the tent out. This is my father's ski. It is a Rossignol. My god, it must be from the seventies. I'm not kidding. He used to be a ski instructor, I think in the seventies or so. He taught me how to ski on the hills around the Twin Cities. When I thought I was good enough, he took me out to Aspen for some spring skiing. He was really cool about it. I was sixteen, and he knew a lot of kids would be out there on spring break. His favorite of the four mountains there was Snowmass. It is the farthest out of town but has the best intermediate skiing. On top of the mountain is the Big Burn. A forest fire took a lot of trees a long time ago, and it has some cool blue runs for me. It makes me laugh when I think of how, when we were in line to get on the chair lift and there were some boys behind me, he would make up some excuse, like he had to adjust his boots, and then he would get out of line, leaving me alone. At first I thought it was strange, but then I figured out the ruse. It wasn't long before I heard *"Single!"* yelled out behind me. I turned around, and three cute boys were yelling "Single!" I chuckled and motioned for the cutest to come and join me on the chairlift.

Father would hop back in at the back of the line. He was always doing things like that to me. After all, who wants to be with an old geezer in the make-out capital of Colorado?

Gustavus Adolphus College is a small Lutheran college

about one hour southwest of the Twin Cities in the little town of St. Peter, Minnesota. It has an enrollment of some two thousand students. It is also fifteen minutes north of Mankato, Minnesota, the site of the largest mass execution in United States history. On December 16, 1862, thirty-eight Dakota were hanged. Rather than hanging them one at a time, a large square scaffold was built with room for ten ropes on each side.

Toward the end of the extermination of the natives of the continent, the survivors were promised land and food in exchange for their surrender. They were confined to small parcels of land that were of no use to the white man. The federal government had promised to supply them with food. White men called Indian agents were selected to see to these matters. But when the meat and food arrived from the government, the Indian agents sold the food and pocketed the money. When the Dakota went to the Indian agent and said that their people had no food and were starving, the Indian agent told them to eat grass. The uprising began, and before it was over, hundreds on both sides lay dead. The Indian agent was found dead on the ground with a piece of sod in his mouth. Three hundred and three Dakota were found guilty of killing whites and sentenced to hang. That number was reduced to thirty-nine and at the last minute, thirty-eight.

On a cold December day, the thirty-eight were led to the scaffold, some with heads down, others with heads held high, singing their "death chant," their leg irons clanking as they climbed the stairs and assumed their final stop. A trumpet blared and drums rolled. As the trapdoors gave way and thirty-eight ropes snapped to attention, the Dakota Uprising came to an end.

I'm standing on the grass by the college. It is a pretty college in a pretty town. This is the college my mother attended. I'm trying to get a feeling. Something. I haven't been here before, but I'm hoping for a nudge or a twinge. I have seen pictures of what the campus was like when my mother was there. But now it is different. In the pictures, the beautiful campus was lined with mature trees. But a few years ago, a tornado tore through the town and downed all the trees on the campus. I mean, all the trees. They've done a good job of replacing the trees, but it's not the same. And there was Dutch elm disease taking the hundred-year-old elms. And now there is the emerald ash borer. It's not the same. Beautiful. But not the same. No nudge. No twinge.

The Flame is a bar in St. Peter, stumbling distance from the campus. It was *the* place to hang out for college kids. When my mother was there, the drinking age was eighteen, and I can imagine the crowds. Now, of course, it is twenty-one; also, it is summer, and the kids, for the most part, have gone home. At twenty-one, I'm the same age as some of the kids who come here. It's not much different from some of the dives we have near campus at the University of Minnesota. The only difference is that this is the only place in town. When my mother was here, they tell me that there was a barn out of town that could be rented out for beer busts. They didn't call it by that name, there was a code name: "barn dance." And there would be "barn dance" postings around campus, and everyone would show up for the beer bust. I asked around to see if I could check it out, but no one now knows anything about it.

So I'm sitting at the bar. I have ordered a beer. I

usually have wine. But I know when my mother was here, everyone ordered the suds. With the tuition of a private school, that's all they could afford. And they would order by the pitcher. I've got a lot of driving to do, so a glass will do just fine, thank you very much.

It's a small place. There are stools at the bar and wooden booths along the wall. I can imagine the atmosphere thirty years or so ago. Wall-to-wall students, beer glasses in hand and pitchers tipped to fill the empties. I can almost hear the din. I smile. I would have liked to come to a college town like this. Be a "Gustie." Have about five hundred students in your class rather than the thousands at the U of M. I chuckle at the thought.

Other than an old man nursing his beer at the end of the bar, I am the only customer. The bartender has been reading a newspaper at the end of the bar by the old man, but he keeps turning his head in my direction. I take a long pull, put the glass down, and shake my head, swishing my hair to the side. The bartender puts the paper down and saunters over to me.

"Are you at the school?" he asks.

"No," I say.

He looks me over. "I don't know," he says. "You look familiar. Have you been in here before?"

"No," I respond.

He shakes his head.

"How long have you been working here?" I ask.

"Oh, I bought the bar, what, maybe thirty some years ago. No, it was more like thirty-five."

"Well, my mother was here back then." I take a swig of beer.

"Well, do you look like her?"

I laugh and choke, and some beer goes up my nose.

"Are you okay?" he asks.

I swallow hard, and breath comes back to me. I look

around the bar, the empty booths that would be filled with college kids, the stools at the bar that would seat those lucky enough to find a seat while they talked to their friends standing next to them. I can imagine the smoke from thirty years ago when it was legal to smoke in bars. I can smell the beer that has spilled on the floor. And I can hear the laughter and pronouncement of the crowd. But no twinge. But maybe it is the bartender that feels the twinge that I am looking for.

"Do I take after my mother?" I repeat the question, smiling. "Yeah, you might say that."

Okay, okay, it's time. I've been to my mother's high school. I've been to her college. I've had beer foam up my nose at her favorite bar. And I've been to the exact spot where my parents announced their engagement to my grandparents. There was something there. Definitely something. I've done all I can here. Now it's time to go. Lisa has taken over my father's agency and is doing well. Andi is in New York. She has a steady relationship with her boyfriend, whom I really like. Jeff and Elizabeth have families and careers and kids. The house is clean and up for sale. It wouldn't be a bad idea for me to just get out.

I've dragged my father's tent up from the basement. It's a big old blue three-man tent. It looks like it's from the last century. Actually, it is. But that's okay. I don't really care how it looks. And I don't really care what other people think about how it looks. If it keeps the rain off, that's all I need. And who knows? I might meet somebody and need a little extra room. Ah, shit, what am I thinking? I really miss Joe. There are times when I feel I should call him up and tell him it was all a mistake and all my fault. But then I think about why I broke up with him. It's not him. It's me. I have to do this. I have to try to find something. I can't do it with him. It is time, to paraphrase Hamlet, to absent myself from felicity a while.

I've got my tent and backpack and I've got my sleeping bag and I've got my cooler and I've got my books. It's time for me to go. But where? My mother has been to Banff, Alberta, twice, and my father has been there three times. Perhaps there is some kind of convergence there. I don't know. All I know is it is time to go.

Chapter 7

THERE IS A KNOCKING.

"Go away."

More knocking.

I move in my sleep. "Go away."

There is a light shining in my face. I wake up. More knocking on the car window. A light from a flashlight is shining on me. I move in my sleeping bag.

"Ma'am," from the other side of the window. "Ma'am, you'll have to open the window."

"Who is it?" I manage.

"Highway Patrol," from outside. "Please open the window."

I'm groggy, and now I see the flashing lights coming from the vehicle parked behind my car. I shake my head. "Just a minute," I say.

"Open the window," again.

I sit up, still in the sleeping bag on the back seat of my car. I move to the window and open it about an inch. "What is it?" I ask. "How do I know you're Highway Patrol?" sleepily.

The flashlight goes to the uniform and the badge, flashes to the patrol car behind me and then back to me. I feel stupid. There is a car with red lights flashing, a man in a uniform with a badge, and I ask, "Who could this be?"

"Ma'am," says the officer. "This is a rest area, not a campground."

"Oh, I'm sorry," I say.

"Ma'am, I'll have to see your license and registration."

My license … let's see. Oh, yeah, it's in my shorts. Let's see. Ah … there it is. I take it from the pocket and bring it up to the window.

"Ma'am, you'll have to get out of the car."

"But I was sleeping, and …" *Oh my god, I've only got a T-shirt and panties on.*

"Ma'am, please step out of the car."

"Wait a minute." I reach for my shorts and slip them on, move over, and open the car door. Stepping out, I hand the officer my driver's license.

"I'll need to see your registration card," says the officer.

I open the front door, slip into the driver's seat, reach across, and open the glove box. Papers fly out. I fumble for a while and finally come up with the card. I step out of the car and hand it to the officer.

I can tell the officer is trying to determine my demeanor and if there is any alcohol on my breath. There isn't.

"Wait here," says the officer and heads for his patrol car. In a few minutes, he returns.

"Everything checks out," he says, handing me back my license and registration.

"I'm sorry, officer," I say. "I tried to get a campsite, but all the campgrounds are full. And I was just so sleepy I was afraid to drive anymore. I can show you my tent in the trunk if you like."

The officer shakes his head. "Nay," he says. "You know you can reserve a campsite, don't you?"

"Well, yeah," I say. "I was actually planning to get to Rapid City tonight, but I stopped at Wounded Knee, and I guess time just got away from me."

"Wounded Knee, eh?"

"Yeah, my father was there quite a while ago, and he told me, that before I die, I should go and see Wounded Knee. So I guess I stayed longer than I had planned."

"Wounded Knee," he says, nodding his head as if he has a secret he is keeping from me. "Go back to sleep," he says. "Just don't be here in the morning."

I'm lying in the back seat of my car. I can't get back to sleep. You can reserve campsites, ya know. You can use a computer or cell phone and put it on your plastic. I have a pretty good idea where I'm going, but I don't really know how I'm going to get there. And that's the way I want it. I want to find something. I want to find myself. But on a journey of discovery, you don't tell the world where you want to go. You want the world to tell you. I want to disconnect from the world I knew, the person I thought I was. I want to find the person I am. You cannot find yourself by a preprogrammed itinerary. You have to ship your oars and set your sail to fate's wind.

I had intended to make it to Rapid City the first day and camp out somewhere around Mount Rushmore. But my father had told me about Wounded Knee battleground.

Chapter 8

I STOOD BEFORE THE MONUMENTS. I STOOD BEFORE THE markers. I stood before the grass that had been stained by the blood of children. I had heard about the massacre. I had read about it. I had read that the last of the Lakota and Hunkpapa Sioux were to be led to the Pine Ridge Indian Reservation, where they would be interned, thus ending the Indian War. And also, perhaps, ending the civilization and culture of the first people of this continent. They made their way to Wounded Knee Creek, where they made camp before the final journey to the Pine Ridge Reservation. But the Seventh Cavalry cut them off. The soldiers surrounded the camp. They brought with them Hotchkiss guns, rapid-firing cannon filled with grapeshot. All the Dakota wanted was to peacefully travel to the reservation, but the general, Nelson Miles, had ordered that the Indians be disarmed. Chief Spotted Elk, wracked with pneumonia, asked that they be allowed to keep their rifles for hunting, as they had no other way to fend for themselves. But the order was given, and several rifles were placed in a pile in the center of the camp. The soldiers went into the tents and found more rifles. There was a struggle with someone, a shot was fired, and the cannons roared. The unarmed Lakota and Hunkpapa were mowed down, heartlessly. Some of the women and children tried to flee, but the mounted soldiers, nostrils filled with victory, chased them down. Most males were killed on the spot, but there were bodies of women and children found two miles from the site. On a cold Dakota field by Wounded Knee Creek, South Dakota, December 29, 1890, the Indian War came to a close.

So, in 1890, the frontier officially came to an end. Frontier. Let me give you a definition of *frontier.* It is land adjacent to yours that you can explore. And if you like it, go ahead and kill the inhabitants and take it for your own.

I sat in the grass; my legs no longer held me up. I have known what it is like to be blindsided. It is nothing like what these people went through. But I sat in the grass, not able to move, wondering how any of the survivors could have gone on. I waited there until the sun was down and the night came upon me like a black sheet. But I was so tired. So tired. I rose, stumbled to my car, and took one last look, trying to find some meaning behind the darkness. Head down, I started the car and headed for the first rest area.

Wall Drug. You've seen the posters. You've seen the bumper stickers. What started out as a simple drugstore off a two-lane road, which is now Interstate 90 on the way to the Black Hills, has turned into a mega-tourist trap. There have been reports of Wall Drug bumper sticker sightings as far away as Australia and Germany. I see a bumper sticker: "I lost my heart at Wall Drug, South Dakota." And another one: "I found my heart at Wall Drug, South Dakota." Sort of a front-bumper, rear-bumper montage, I suppose. It's kind of fun actually, if you make the stop. I think I'll pick up a bumper sticker as long as I'm here. I'll probably need it the next time I'm in Portugal.

Chapter 9

THIS IS MY CAMPSITE. THIS IS *MY* CAMPSITE. IT'S NOT WHAT I wanted, but it will do. I wanted a more private campsite. Sort of in-the-woods type of campsite. But this is more like a community. I have a separate campsite, but it is not too far away from my neighbors. I can hear them when they are talking. There is music from a campsite down the way, which is bullshit. There are some trees. But nothing like a forest. No loose firewood that you could scrounge for. No. If you want a fire, you have to go up to the store and buy a bundle. And along the way, you can pass a camper with an "If this trailer's rockin', don't bother knockin'" sticker on it.

The store has some amenities. You can get some canned food if you're hungry enough. And it has beer and wine if you're thirsty enough. So I bought the best bottle of wine that they had for fifteen dollars. It's been in my cooler for an hour or so, so it should be ready. It rained earlier today, and the firewood was wet. I saw some clown down the block, so to speak, throw some gasoline on a pile of wood and throw a match to it. What a *whoosh*. He jumped back and tripped over the tongue of his trailer, spilling his can of beer. I laughed out loud.

My tent is my father's big blue nylon three-person tent. It looks too big and clumsy. No serious camper would use a tent like this. But this is not a serious campground. This is a campground for latecomers or people who don't care. Like I don't care. It was good enough for my father, and it's good enough for me. Wherever I go, this will be my home. Maybe I'll need the room. Maybe I'll meet a lonesome hunk who needs a ride. And maybe needs a bed. Who knows? I'm on a grand adventure. Leave the one-man tents to the serious campers. I'll be serious enough in my big blue house of a tent, my "Big Blue."

I went into the "woods" for a while and scrounged up quite a few pine needles. I set the wood in a pile away from my tent and took out my hatchet. With my hatchet, I shaved off quite a bit of kindling from a piece of pine log. I placed the pine needles in a small pile and placed the kindling on top. I split a couple of logs with my hatchet into some smaller pieces of wood. The interior of the wood was dry. Going to my camp bag, I pulled out a candle. I cut an inch off the top and put the rest back in my pack. The inch of candle went beneath the pine needles and kindling, and some smaller logs went on top. Paraffin from the candle will burn even when it is wet. I lit the candle, and as soon as I saw smoke from the pine needles, I went to work blowing from the side. It wasn't long before I had a nice campfire, no match, no paper. So ... I cheated a little with the candle. Hey, this is my very first campsite by myself. It had rained, all the wood was wet, and I, a single female, had the best campfire in the campground. Chew on that, Mr. "If This Trailer's Rockin', Don't Bother Knockin'."

I took the wine bottle from the cooler, opened it, and poured myself a glass. I sat down on the ground as the sun set. My tent was up, my campfire was burning, and I had a glass of wine in my hand. I turned around to Big Blue. "I can do this," I said. "I really can do this."

I'm lying in my sleeping bag with Big Blue. The wine has taken effect, and I feel mellow. I don't hear much from the other campers. There were some being rowdy before. But now the fires have dwindled, and I think someone has retired and is tryin' to start the trailer rockin'. Good luck with that.

Anyway, I've got Big Blue to keep me company. He just asked me why I had to break up with Joe. I didn't need to genderize him, but this is Dad's old tent, and I thought it best to think of it as a him. Besides, I need someone to talk to. And right now, I'd rather talk to a man.

So why did I have to break up with Joe? Joe loved me. Maybe he still does. I think I still love him. But he couldn't go with me on this trip. I have to find something. I don't even know what I'm looking for. But I know I can't find it with Joe.

The question is, Who am I? Am I Chloe? Am I my mom, Jenny? Perhaps I'm both. Perhaps I'm neither. I have always known myself as I grew up. But I never knew Jenny. She is the same as me. The identical same as me. Would she be thinking the same things I'm thinking? We have different experiences in life, and maybe we would be thinking different thoughts about different things. But if we had the same experiences, would we be thinking of the same thing? They say that identical twins can feel each other's thoughts. But I am not a twin. I don't know who I am. I don't know what I am. So I tell Big Blue that the things I need to find, the things I need to know, I have to do myself. And I will find them by myself. I'm not concerned. I'm here with Big Blue. At least I'm not alone.

Chapter 10

THE BADLANDS OF THE DAKOTAS ARE APTLY NAMED. NOT much grows here. Just prairie dogs popping their heads out of the ground. They are fun to watch, standing at attention. You can get quite close to them before they pop down, only to reappear at a safer distance. There is some game here to hunt, but you have to be very patient. Theodore Roosevelt spent a lot of time in the northern Badlands near Medora, North Dakota. He came out here for medical reasons and got to love the wildness of it. Boy, did it fit his disposition.

Although it is stark and desolate, it is beautiful. There are multicolored striations in the mounds and hills that have been eroded through the centuries. Dinosaurs once roamed this land, and if you dig around enough, you may find a bone or two. But digging is forbidden here, except for true paleontologists. But some people will always carve something into the rock: maybe a name, maybe something else.

I went off the highway onto a dirt road. There were quite a few prairie dogs looking at me when I stopped the car. I took some bread and got out of the car. I thought it would be nice to share. I know it's not right to feed the wild, but I could use the company right now—to be close to an innocent, warm-blooded animal and share a repast. Besides, they're cute. *Come here, little prairie dog. Let me pet you. Let me hold in my hands, something warm and soft and innocent that I can give some love to. I need to give some love. And I need to be loved back.* But the prairie dog will have none of it. As I get close, it just turns its back and scuffles into its hole. The feelings that I have now—is this what Joe felt? Is this what Joe is feeling? He would give his love to me, and I have stonewalled him. No explanation. It's like I just turned off the lights. God, I miss him. God, I wish I could go back and take him in my arms and tell him that it was all a mistake. Tell him to just wipe it from his memory as if it never happened.

That would never happen. And shouldn't happen. That would be unfair to the man I still love. I can go back, but I can't tell him why I left. Would he understand if I did? Or would he throw me under the bus? I wouldn't blame him if he did.

What I did to him was unfair. But it was necessary. I'm not the person I thought I was, and I am not the person he thought I was. I may go back and see him again. But I can't go back until I find myself.

The Black Hills are beautiful. Just west of the Badlands, the pine forests make the landscape appear black, with some large rocks exploding from the ground. The name "Black Hills" comes from the Lakota, one of the three tribes of the Sioux Nation. It means "hills that are black." It is a sacred place for the Lakota. It was used as a place where natives could come to seek visions or to purify themselves. It was considered a sanctuary and peaceful meeting ground for the Native Americans. Safety was guaranteed for anyone coming there with peaceful intentions. However, General George Custer led an army exploration into the area in 1874. Gold was discovered, and more whites soon followed. The Native Americans who cherished the area were pushed out. Two years later, General George Armstrong Custer would have a different meeting with the natives.

You've seen the pictures. Presidents' heads inscribed in rock. But you are not prepared. When you round a curve in the road—there they are in the distance. They are far away, and they are huge. Another curve, and they are gone from sight. And then you round another corner, and there they are. I was not prepared. Didn't crash the car. But could have; I was staring at the sight.

I parked the car in the parking lot, got out, and walked to a standing station in front of this edifice, this monument. The pictures do not do it justice. It is huge! Four faces, locked together in stone: George Washington, Thomas Jefferson, Theodore Roosevelt, and Abraham Lincoln. Huge piles of stone detritus lie at the bottom, below the figures. You wonder how anyone could create such a marvelous sculpture. I mean, this is just stone. This is a mountain. I just stood there, amazed at the grandeur. It was first envisioned by a South Dakota senator, Peter Norbeck, in 1924 as a way to get tourists to come from around the country. It was also intended to carve figures of Native Americans out of the stone. But sculptor Gutzon Borglum had other ideas. He chose the four presidents to represent what he thought of as leaders and preservers of this country.

A few miles down the road from Mount Rushmore is the Crazy Horse memorial. It is amazing. When it is done, Crazy Horse will be on his horse, pointing to the east. Apparently, it is in response to a white man's question: "Where are your lands?" To which the Ogallala Sioux warrior replied, "My lands are where my dead are buried," signifying the westward push of the white man and the carnage they left as they went.

When finished, this will be the largest sculpture in the world, dwarfing Mount Rushmore. It will be larger than the pyramid at Giza and three times as high as Niagara Falls. There are plans to have a lake around it with sailboats and the like, but I'll never live to see it. The creators have refused government funding, so the process is painstakingly slow.

But it *is* a process, and I am glad that we are finally paying homage to the people who lived on this land until they were decimated by an avalanche of treachery, annihilation, and power. The Great Sioux Nation, which covered a large portion of this continent, basing their values on family, fairness, justice, and truth, has been reduced to small pockets. And all they have left to show of their great societies and culture is a pocketful of casinos and a warrior made of stone.

I left Crazy Horse behind. On my way west, I got off Interstate 90 onto Highway 14, which in turn turned onto Highway 24 by the Belle Fourche River. I'm going to Devils Tower. You may have seen it in the movie, *Close Encounters of the Third Kind*. The aliens picked a very alien-looking place to land.

Some people think it is what is left of a volcano. But it isn't. Millions of years ago, magma welled up into the surrounding sedimentary rock and cooled. Over time, the surrounding rock fell off, exposing solidified magma that looks like rock tubes reaching skyward. It is a magnificent and magical sight. You may never see anything like it on this continent. And it was a magical place for the Lakota Sioux, who considered it sacred. It was a place where they would allow travelers from other tribes to come into their territory to seek the Great Spirit.

I am back in the plains again, and I can see it from quite a distance. As I drive to it, prairie dogs pop their heads up as I pass. I stop in the parking area and get out. Many people mill around this huge monument to nature's eccentricity and whimsy. To give you some idea of its grandeur, it is 867 feet from the base to the summit and a mile around at its circumference. The trail around it, where people like me go, adds another one-third mile.

There is awe in this giant obelisk. You can almost feel the spirits that the natives sought. It is here they came to seek the spirits, free themselves from their unholiness, or find the path that they were made to follow. I hop in my car. As I drive down the road, a sea of prairie dogs has emerged from their holes, standing upright, craning their necks to see this freak of un-nature. And as I drive by, rows of prairie dogs, perpendicular to my passing car, pop into their holes, only to reemerge behind me. It's as if the spirits of this holy land have summoned them and, with this wave, send me on my way.

Well, I'm off to the Little Bighorn battlefield. I've always wanted to visit there. A real battlefield. To just stand there and envision the battle. And I've heard that there is a special ceremony every year in June, some sort of a reenactment. Well, it's June. Let's see what there is to see.

Chapter 11

A Fight That You Will Lose

If you visit Montana in the summer, you will have the opportunity to visit the Little Bighorn Battlefield National Monument. Located sixty miles southeast of Billings, it straddles the Little Bighorn River. You can actually stand on the bluffs overlooking the battlefield and see white markers in the distance. Close to you are a couple of white markers signifying where two soldiers were found. A little farther up are three or four white markers. Single markers are scattered about, and a little farther up the hill are quite a few markers, in the midst of which is a monument signifying where Custer's body was found. You may never have stood on an actual battlefield before. But here you can stand and, with the aid of the markers, visualize the battle. You can imagine Custer splitting the Seventh Regiment. Major Reno was to cross the river downstream and attack the Indians, forcing them northward, where they would be met by Custer's men. You can see Custer bring his troops along the ridgeline and attack down the hill to the river, be repulsed, and retreat back up the bluffs to make his last stand against the "savages."

And if you are lucky enough to be there on June 25, you can go down to the other side of the river and hear the battle from another point of view. Every June 25, Native Americans set up camp on the very ground that held their teepees on June 25, 1876. You can walk around the village and enter the teepees. Later, you can sit in the bleachers that they have erected and listen to their story. They will tell you what it was like before the white man came. They will tell you that they had many battles among themselves. Two ponies carrying young Indians will race through the camp. One will catch the other and touch him, and they will ride off. The speaker will explain that the most powerful thing a warrior can do is to touch his enemy without hurting him. A canoe will appear around a bend in the river and come ashore at river's edge in front of you. Two men and a woman in buckskin will get out of the canoe and walk toward the bleachers. The speaker explains that these people are Lewis and Clark and Sacagawea, and that the Indians helped the white men as they first came onto their land. On the horizon, you see a group of mounted cavalry riding the ridge overlooking the river. They wear the blue shirts of the Seventh Cavalry, and the leader has a blond beard and long blond hair and wears a tan buckskin jacket: Custer. Custer and his men charge down the bluffs, guns ablaze, only to be repulsed and forced back up the slope by men defending their women and children. A melee ensues, with rifles and pistols firing, and then all is silent. The blue coats and the tan buckskin are down. The speaker explains that they are here to honor the warriors of this battle. But they are not here to honor just the brave men that died on this battlefield: the Cheyenne, Sans Aves, Sioux, Blackfoot, and Hunkpapa. They are here to honor the fallen from all wars. They are here to honor the Native American men and women who fell for their country in World War II. And they are here to honor those that did not come back from Korea. And they are here to honor those that died in a faraway place called Vietnam. For although they are proud of their Native American heritage, they consider themselves Americans. You sit on a flat bench in the bleachers and wonder how a people who had their land taken from them, a people who were rounded up and put on barren land called reservations, a people who, when starving, were told to eat grass, a people who had every promise made to them broken and were brought to the brink of annihilation, could call themselves Americans.

They pass out two small flags to each of you. And you hold the two flags in your hand. You see that one flag is an American flag and the other is a flag with two hands clasped together in the fellowship of humanity. You feel your throat tighten. And you fight to hold back the tears. But it is a fight that you will lose.

Chapter 12

I HAVE WIPED AWAY THE TEARS FROM MY EYES, BUT SMALL teardrops mark my T-shirt. I can see okay, and I can drive. I point my car down the dirt road, carved from the grasslands that head away from the battlefield. I turn onto pavement and make my way toward Highway 90, which should take me past Billings and on to the mountains. As I approach the freeway, a man in a hat stands by the road with his hand stuck out, thumb extended. He has a backpack with a sleeping bag and tent. Right now, my kind of guy. My dad would tell me not to pick up strangers. But I'm feeling kind of wistful. I could use some company right now. If I don't feel comfortable, I can make up some excuse and let him off down the road.

I pull the car over, just past where he was standing. He picks up his gear and trundles to the car. I roll the window down. "Where you goin'?" I ask.

"West," the young man says. He is quite good-looking: tanned face, blue eyes, six feet one maybe, 170 pounds. His backpack is topped with rollups tied down with bungee cords: two nylon, probably sleeping bag and one-man tent, and a rolled-up thin rubber sleeping mat. I have a three-man tent and a blow-up air mattress. I don't mind sleeping on the ground. But not the ground-ground.

"Throw your gear in the back and hop in," I say.

He opens the rear passenger door, tosses in his gear, and closes the rear door.

I have already reached over and pushed the passenger door open. He hops in and closes the door. "Billy," he says.

"Hi, I'm Chloe," I return, extending my hand.

He shakes my hand, and we're on the freeway heading west.

"Thanks," he says. "It's tough catching a ride these days."

"I imagine," I say.

"There was a time," he says. "A time where one could hitch right on the Interstate. At least, it was easier. But now we have to catch a ride on a road less traveled and see where it goes." As he pulls off his hat, a cascade of black hair falls from underneath. He shakes his head like a wet dog, to loosen whatever knots have formed.

"Nice hair," I say.

"Thanks," he says and looks at me. "You too."

I laugh. "Yeah," I say. I have to keep my eyes on the road, but I steal a glance at him. He has a very nice face. And, from what I can see, a very nice body. I accelerate and enter the Interstate. "How far west?" I ask as I bring it up to the posted.

"Can't say," he says. "But I hope to know when I get there."

We're past Billings now, heading west on the Interstate. "Where are you headed?" asks Billy.

I feel comfortable with him. He has been with me for a couple of hours now. He is a free talker, but not pushy or dominant in conversation. I have found out that he is from the Twin Cities, as am I. He is from St. Paul.

I am from across the river, Minneapolis side. He likes the Vikings. I like the Twins. He likes the Wild hockey team. I like the Lynx women's basketball. I don't think I'll be pulling over anytime soon to let him out. I feel comfortable with him, and I could use the company.

"Pretty much the same as you," I say. "West."

"Break up with your boyfriend?" he asks somewhat hesitantly.

"That's a pretty personal question," I say.

"Sorry," he says.

"Nah," I say. "No, I mean yes, I did break up with my boyfriend. But that's not the reason I am here."

"Wanna talk about it?"

I shake my head. "Not really."

"Cool," he says.

We drive on in silence for another ten minutes or so.

"You planning on staying on the Interstate?" he asks.

"Oh, I don't know," I say. "Never been here before. Suggestions?"

"Well," he says. "Interstate will certainly get you wherever sooner. But I think off-road will get you there better."

"You know a route?"

He leans over the back of his seat and pulls a map from his backpack. Opening it up and perusing it a moment, he says, "If we take the Interstate up to Butte and turn north onto 15, it will take us up to Lewis and Clark National Forest. It might be faster to stay on the freeways, but it's not as pretty."

"Any alternate routes?" I ask.

"Hopin' you'd say that," he says. "Cut off on 98 just before Bozeman, left on 12, which will take us around Canyon Ferry Lake. We may want to stop and take a look. And it'll be about an hour and half from there."

"Been there?"

"Yup," he says. "Most of the campgrounds these days, you need reservations. And most of the campsites are filled up long in advance, mostly by people who have an agenda or planned route. If you are just flying with the wind, it's better to find campgrounds that don't take resos and get there early. I think there are about five campgrounds there, and none of them take resos. So we might want to wander up there and see what they have. We should get there around dinner time."

I do not respond.

"Oh shit," he says. "That's a little forward of me. I mean, camping together and all. We'll have separate tents."

I shrug my shoulders.

"Look," he said. "If you don't feel comfortable sharing a campsite, I'll get a second campsite. Or maybe just head out into the woods."

I turn and take a look at him. He looks back at me with those clear blue eyes, long black hair, and square shoulders. "Highway 89, two tents," I say and turn back to the highway.

We make a stop at Canyon Ferry Lake. It's a big lake. Pretty. But all lakes in the mountains are pretty. This is just a dammed-up Missouri River lake. I prefer the spring-fed lakes a little higher up. At least from the pictures I've seen.

We continue to the town of Augusta and hang a left, and we are in the mountains. I mean, shit, we are in the Rocky Mountains. The Spine of the Continent. Billy knows the way and directs me to the campground pay station. We park the car and go inside. Billy walks over to the man at the counter. "We'd like a campsite," he says.

The man looks up from his paper and looks us over. "Room with a view?" he asks.

Billy chuckles. "Yeah," he says to the man. "Room with a view."

The man takes out a map of the campground and turns it toward Billy as I mosey up beside him. The man points at a campsite along the river. "You're in luck," he says. "No one has taken it yet."

"Great," says Billy. "How much?"

The man points at the chart on the wall. "Six bucks," he says.

"Oh, by the way," says Billy. "We have two tents. If it's more money ..."

"Is one big enough for both of you?" asks the man.

"Well, yeah," Billy says. "But ..."

I hold up two fingers.

The man looks at Billy—then to me—back to Billy. "Six bucks," he says and turns back to his paper.

So, I'm lying in my tent, old Big Blue. Got my ancient sleeping bag and my blow-up air mattress. I must say I think I heard a slightly suppressed giggle from Billy when I was pumping it up. But hey, I'm new to this, and I'm tryin'. I'm here, ain't I?

This is a really good campsite. It normally holds only one tent the size of mine, but Billy's is a one-man tent, a really small one-man tent. I look at Big Blue and then back to Billy's tent.

"Kind of a small tent," I say.

Billy shrugs. "Big enough for one," he says. "Or maybe two. If they are intimate, really intimate, and no one farts."

I laugh. He's a good-looking young man. He told me

about himself. He's half Indian ... make that half Native American. His mother was white, and his father was from a reservation southeast of the Twin Cities. His father was killed in a car accident when he was very young. His mother raised him in the Cities, but she made sure that he was aware of his Native American heritage. Every summer, he would stay with his uncle, Red Eagle, on the reservation. There he learned hand-to-hand combat, Native American tracking skills, and something about living with animals. He called it "whispering." He showed me an eagle feather that he always has with him. It is his most prized possession, sort of a good luck charm, I guess. One interesting thing about him is that he has beautiful blue eyes. I know that brown eyes are dominant in Native Americans and that usually carries over to their offspring. Not this time. His mother was Danish. Luck of the draw, I guess.

We pitched our tents, or should I say, Billy pitched his tent, and as I put up Big Blue, he was already back from the woods with firewood. The site overlooks the north fork of the Teton River on one side and a magnificent view of the Sawtooth Range on the other side. Billy had bought a six-pack of Coors when we stopped at the lake, and I had another bottle of Chardonnay from my stash. We hiked down to river's edge and skipped rocks while the entertainment cooled in the ice chest.

I can hear a slight snore outside. And I wonder what it would be like. He is in his tent. I am in mine. My tent is big enough. What am I thinking? I just met this guy. I didn't pick him up. I just offered him a ride. It's nice to have a companion. That's all. Just for a while. And he knows the area. He knows the campsites. He did not make any moves or anything. Just an intelligent, easygoing, good-looking companion for a while. Did I mention that he is good-looking? I hope he's not gay. What the hell am I thinking? What difference would it make? We're not going to do anything. Just a companion. Just a guy to, maybe, show me some things. But I do like his hair. Sort of wild thing. Yes, definitely the hair. Did I tell you that he took off his shirt at the river? Yup, six-pack and shoulders. Not overdone. Kind of like what I've seen in some magazines. Yeah, I've looked at some studs in some magazines, and just for a moment, I wondered what it would be like. You know, out in the wilderness with this, ah ... No! Chloe, pivot! Let's see, ah ... It was a nice drive. Um ... The campsite is beautiful. Skipping stones at the river was fun. Or should I say, watching Billy skip stones was fun. Campfire was warm, and the wine was good. Nothing happened. Nothing is going to happen. That's right! I'll just lie here in my sleeping bag and nod off to sleep. And in the morning, we'll head out again. I'll just think of something else as I lie and listen to the slight snore. The slight, manly snore from outside my tent.

Chapter 13

WE'VE MADE IT UP TO BROWNING, JUST EAST OF GLACIER National Park. We've checked ahead, and all the campgrounds are full. We've decided we might as well have a bite to eat and check around to see if anyone will let us pitch out tents on their land. We're at a table in Bunny's Bar. Billy has ordered a beer, and I will have the house wine and hope. We ask the waitress if she knows anyone who would let us park on their land. She points to the bartender and says, "Ask Bunny. He might know someone."

I look to the bar, and there is a big guy, orca big, pouring a drink. "Bunny?" I ask.

The waitress nods. "Bunny knows everyone around here," she says. "I'm sure he can fix you up."

We both saunter up to the bar. Billy takes the lead. "I understand you're Bunny," he says.

Bunny finishes with the drink and says, "Yeah" as he hands it to the patron sitting next to us.

"The waitress said you might be able to help us," says Billy.

"Sure," says Bunny. "Whatdaya need?"

"Well," starts Billy. "The campgrounds are all full, and we need a place to camp. We were wondering if you knew someone who would let us set up our tents on their land. We would pay, of course."

Bunny puts two beefy hands on the bar. "Like your hair," he says to Billy. "Where you from?"

"We're from Minnesota, just camping out," Billy manages.

Bunny keeps looking at Billy's hair. "You Injun?" he asks.

"Half," says Billy.

Bunny nods his head. "Minnesota," he says. "Let's see, Sioux?"

Billy nods. "Yeah, Dakota."

"Well," says Bunny. "This is Blackfoot country."

"Right," says Billy.

Bunny hesitates for a moment, considering. "There's an elder who has a trailer up 464 a ways, owns the land," he says. "He'd probably help. He's just an elder, but likes to be called Chief. You finish your dinner. I'll call him and tell him you're comin'."

"Thanks," we say in unison and turn toward our table.

"Oh, one thing," says Bunny. "You won't have to pay him money. That would be an insult. Pint of blackberry brandy would do."

I give Bunny a quizzical look.

"That thing about Injuns and liquor is bullshit," says Bunny. "They just like anyone else. You go finish your dinner. I'll call him and tell him you're comin'."

I ring the doorbell. A large man opens the door. His long, gray hair is pulled back into a ponytail. White shirt open at the neck displays a ring of beads. Worn blue jeans with a cowboy belt buckle and cowboy boots. "Heard you were comin'," he says.

"We were hoping that you would let us pitch our tents

on your land," I say and pull the bottle of brandy from the paper bag. "We offer you a gift in exchange for letting us sleep on your land for one night." I hold out the bottle. "We'll be gone in the morning."

Chief takes the bottle, examining it. "Blackberry brandy," he says.

"Yes," I say. "They said we should bring a gift and that you would like blackberry brandy."

Chief unscrews the top of the bottle and brings it to his nose to sniff. "You know that thing about Indians not being able to handle their liquor," he says. "That's just bullshit."

"That's what I've heard," says Billy.

Chief looks Billy over. "Where you from?" he asks.

"Minnesota," says Billy.

"You Injun?" asks Chief.

"Half," says Billy.

"Half?" asks Chief. "Sioux? Ojibwa?"

"Sioux. My father was Dakota," answers Billy.

Chief nods. "You know, Blackfoot and Sioux used to fight a lot."

"Guess so," says Billy.

"But that was mainly the Lakota Sioux," says Chief. "Not Dakota." Chief looks to the ground for a moment. "But that was long ago."

"Yeah," says Billy. "A long time ago."

"What's your name?" asks Chief.

"Billy Simpson," says Billy.

"You got an Injun name?"

"Yeah," says Billy. "Growing up, I spent my summers on the reservation. My given name is Two Bears. It was given to me by my uncle, Red Eagle. He is an elder in the tribe."

"Did he teach you anything?" asks Chief.

"He taught me how to hunt and how to track and how to fight," says Billy.

A smile appears on Chief's face.

"And I got this," says Billy, pulling an eagle feather from beneath his shirt.

"You got that by yourself?"

"Yes," says Billy.

"And the eagle, does it still fly?" asks Chief.

Billy nods. "It still flies," he says.

The smile on Chief's face widens. Chief puts the cap back on the bottle and looks at me. "Tents?" he asks.

"Yes," I say. "We each have our own tent."

"One tent," says Chief.

"But we just met ..." I start.

Chief looks at the bottle and nods. "One bottle." He points to a spot in front of the mobile home and says, "One tent."

"What's with the feather?" I ask as we roll out our sleeping bags in Big Blue, his on the left side, mine on the right—the far right. There is no center pole, as guy lines pull the tent poles apart, creating an open space throughout the tent that is illuminated by our two flashlights. The space between us will be a dead zone in the middle so I can intercept any creeping hands.

"It's an eagle feather," says Billy.

"Yes, I could see that," I say. "But why did Chief smile when you said the eagle still flies?"

"Well," says Billy as he fluffs his sleeping bag. "There are two ways one can obtain an eagle feather. One is to pick it off the ground or take it from a dead bird on the ground. And the other is to take it from a live bird in the wild."

"What are you talking about?" I ask incredulously.

"Taking it from a bird in the wild. Taking it with your bare hands."

"You're joking."

Billy shakes his head. "No. No joke."

I close my eyes in disbelief. Opening them, I say, "You took a feather from a live eagle?"

Billy nods.

"I don't understand," I continue. "How?"

Billy puts his sleeping bag down. "This is not something I brag about," he says. "It's just something I did."

I shake my head and raise my brow. "But I don't know how anyone could do that," I say.

"Well," says Billy. "Maybe I'll tell you sometime. When we get to know each other a little better."

I'm back at shaking the wrinkles out of my sleeping bag. "Promise?" I ask.

Billy starts to take off his clothes, shirt first. He sits on his sleeping bag and takes off his shoes and socks. Then his pants are off, leaving him in just his skivvies. *You can stop there,* I think, perilously close to blurting it out loud. And he does and slithers into his bag. When you have a car, you can bring a pillow. When you are hitchin,' a pillow takes up useable room. Billy folds his pants and shirt and places them below his head as a pillow.

I unzip my sleeping bag and, fully clothed, slide into it. Billy reaches out and turns off his flashlight. Mine is still lighting the back of the tent. I zip my bag over halfway up. I undo my pants, slide them off, and pull them out of the bag. I reach over and turn off my flashlight. My T-shirt is quickly off and out of my bag. I don't like sleeping with my bra on, but I'll make an exception here. My head is barely on my pillow when I hear faint snores across the tent. And I can't help but wonder what it would be like to be with a man who could take a feather from an eagle in the wild.

Chapter 14

I AM AWAKE. I TURN OVER AND SLEEPY EYES SHOW THAT Billy's sleeping bag is gone. As are his flashlight and duffel bag. I unzip my bag. My T-shirt is quickly over my head, and my pants are on. I poke my head out of Big Blue. Billy is fully clothed, sitting on his duffel, looking at the sunrise. "Oh," I blurt out unexpectedly. Billy turns to me.

"Morning," he says. "Sleep okay?"

"Yeah," I manage. "Be with you in a minute."

I pop back in the tent and put my socks and shoes on. I'd really like to lie down and lounge for a while. Ya know, like I was home or something. Billy is up, and I don't think I'd feel right just lyin' around. Especially on someone else's land. So I pack up my stuff and crawl out of the tent.

Billy turns and watches me as I rise to the occasion. "I've got some freeze-dried and a burner in my bag, if you like," he says. "It's such a beautiful morning, and I could sit and watch the sky for a while. But I don't like to lollygag on someone else's land too long. What say we go into town and I will buy you a breakfast?"

Ah, yeah, I think. *Breakfast with the eagle man—that would be cool.*

"Yeah, Billy," I say. "That would be great. I'll get my things, and we can break down the tent."

The tent is quickly down and in the trunk with the sleeping bags. I look again at the beautiful sunrise. Then I turn and move to the mobile home.

"Where you goin'?" asks Billy.

"I thought I'd knock on Chief's door and thank him before we leave."

"You see how he looked at the bottle?" says Billy. "If he drank all of his medicine last night, and I have every reason to think that he did, letting him sleep in will be thanks enough."

I laugh, nod, turn around, and head for the car.

As I drive toward town and breakfast, I look over at Billy in the passenger seat. He is looking out the window. He has his side window rolled down, and his hair wafts in the breeze. There is something about him. He looks so ... I don't know ... so clean. He has not bathed today. For that matter, neither have I. But he just has a feeling of peace around him. He is so comfortable. So at peace with nature. That's the way I want to be. I want to be at peace with nature. I want to be one with nature. I want to be natural. I'm not, and I know it. I am manufactured. Someone has pieces of this and pieces of that and puts them together in a dish, mixes it up, and I come out. Maybe I am natural. Maybe the pieces in the dish are natural, and that makes me natural. But the pieces are not delivered in the natural way. I am not natural. That is why I am here, in this car, with this man, this natural man, sitting next to me. Maybe I can be like him. Maybe I can be at peace with myself. Maybe I can learn. Maybe I can just look out the window and smile at nature. And if I stare long enough, maybe nature will smile back at me. I roll down the side window, and my hair wafts in the fresh, cool breeze. And I feel my lips curl, just a bit.

We're sitting in a booth at a diner. An older couple is down a few booths, and an old man is sitting at the counter. Billy has ordered two slices of toast, a glass of orange juice, and a banana. I ordered a bowl of oatmeal and orange juice. The waitress comes with the food. The pretty young girl asks if we need anything else. We demur and thank her. As Billy starts in on his toast, I hold my hands over the steaming bowl. It was a little cold in the car with the windows down. Don't get me wrong—it was worth it. Billy with his hair flapping and my hair fluffing in the cool morning breeze as we drove, damn the torpedoes.

But I'm a little chilled, and the steam rising from the bowl feels good on my hands.

"You get cold?" asks Billy, looking at my hands.

"Nah," I say. "Just a little."

"Well," says Billy, "that porridge will warm you up."

"Yeah," I say, looking into his blue eyes. "You got blue eyes," I say.

Billy smiles. "Yes, I do," he says.

"I thought ..."

"Yeah, I know," says Billy. "Brown eyes are dominant in Native Americans."

He shakes his head, and black hair flows around his head. "Ya know, I like the term 'Native American,' but it does get somewhat cumbersome at times. I'm glad they are finally giving some recognition to the, ah ... native people here. But I might just slip into saying Injun or Indian. It really doesn't offend me. Hell, Columbus missed his destination by a whole continent."

"And a whole ocean," I add.

Billy laughs. "Yeah," he says. "I'm half white and half Injun. I know that brown eyes are dominant, but my mother's side won out here. And I have blue eyes. It happens."

"Tell me about the feather," I say.

Billy takes a bit of toast and washes it down with a swig of OJ. "My mom raised me," Billy continues, avoiding the question. "She was white, and I grew up in St. Paul." One last bite of toast and another swig. "My father was from the Mdewakanton Dakota Reservation near Red Wing. They got together somehow, and I am here."

"Do you see your dad?" I ask.

"Nah," says Billy. "He died in a car accident when I was young. I never really knew him."

"That's tough," I say.

"Yeah," says Billy. "But my mother was a good woman. And she wanted me to know who I am. So, in the summers, I stayed with my uncle on the reservation. He taught me a lot about the Indian ways. Oops."

I laugh.

"Anyway," continues Billy, "I spent every summer growing up on the reservation. My uncle, Red Eagle, my father's brother, sort of took me in and taught me many things."

"Like what?"

"Well," says Billy tossing his hair again. "He taught me how to track. He taught me how to hunt. And he taught me how to fight. And he taught me some of the Native American ways, and their philosophy of life."

Billy picks up a banana and starts to peel it.

"Tell me about their, or maybe I should say your, philosophy of life."

Billy takes a bite and takes a deep breath as he chews. "My philosophy of life," he says. He waits for a minute and takes another bite of the banana. "I guess I'm trying to find that out myself," he says.

It didn't take long to drive from Browning to Glacier National Park. We got there in plenty of time to find a campsite. We chose Many Glacier campground. There are a lot of campsites near St. Mary's Lake, a large, somewhat narrow lake on the east side of Glacier National Park. Very popular. But those campsites are mainly for trailers and such and, quite frankly, not very attractive. At least, not what I was looking for. Billy told me about a tent-only campground, Many Glacier campground, that was the most scenic campground he had seen. *Now you're talkin'.* We got there early enough to get a good campsite. Just take US Highway 89 to Babb, hang a left onto Many Glacier Road, and after quite a long and scenic ride past Lake Sherburne, you arrive at Swiftcurrent Lake and the campground. It is the best campground that I have ever seen, with glaciers and lakes and trees, oh, my. And it has showers!

Although it is one of the best-kept secrets in camping, you still have to get there early to get a site. And we did.

Billy directs me to a campsite at the far west of the campground. "There's a small lake, Fishercap Lake, over there," he says pointing west of the site. I pull the car into the site. "There's the big lake, Swiftcurrent Lake, back a bit, but that's quite a hike. And I like Fishercap Lake better. It's smaller and doesn't get the foot traffic that Swiftcurrent does. It's small and pretty and peaceful and close." Billy gets out of the car and pulls his pack from the back seat. "This looks good," he says and drops his tent on the ground. "Campsite's big enough for two tents."

I pull Big Blue from the back seat and lay it in the middle of the campsite. I look around at the beautiful mountains and glaciers and trees. The sun is brilliant in the big blue sky. The air has a dry, cool freshness, and when I take a breath, I smell the true mountain air. I turn and look at Billy fiddling with his tent. He has stripped off his shirt, and in the sunlight, I can see his chiseled chest as he works his tent. I'm happy I found him. Or did he find me? Without him, I wouldn't have found this campsite. I wouldn't have found Chief or slept on a reservation. I wonder what else there is in store for me. But there is one thing that I know. I have to find out more about this tall, dark man with long black hair and washboard abs.

"Billy," I say, "Why don't you pack up your tent?"

Billy turns and looks at me.

"Why burden the ground with two tents?" I say.

Chapter 15

AFTER BIG BLUE IS UP AND STOCKED WITH SLEEPING BAGS, we head down to Fishercap Lake. It's not too far. The trail ends at the water. It is a beautiful sight. The water is blue with a green tint. Billy says it is from the glacial silt. There are mountains all around. Billy says they are glaciers, but I can't tell the difference. I thought that glaciers were the ones with snow on them, but most of the mountains around here have snow on them. Whatever they are, they are beautiful. The sky is deep blue, dotted with small, white, puffy clouds. Billy walks a bit down the shoreline and stoops to pick up a stone. As I follow him, he deftly flings the rock into the lake. I try to count the skips, but past ten, I lose count. I lean down and pick up a stone. I try to emulate Billy, but the stone just plops into the water. Billy laughs. I pick up another and try it. Plop. Another laugh from the sidelines. Billy comes over to me, leans down, and picks up another stone.

"Picking the right stone is the first thing you do," he says, holding his stone-laden hand out. "It doesn't have to be perfectly flat, but the flatter, the better." He takes sort of a pitcher stance and side-winds it into the lake, skipping it umpteen times. He reaches into the water and pulls out another stony masterpiece. "Here," he says. He hands me the stone, and I start my girly windup.

"Whoa," he says dramatically, grabbing my arm. "You

can't skip a stone with an overhand delivery." He fakes throwing a stone in slow motion so I can get the picture. "You've got to go side-arm, and get down next to the water with your arm and hand," he says, showing me again.

I try to take a stance, and he stops me. "Let me see your grip," he says. I hold out my hand to him. "No," he says. "You're holding it like a baseball. Curl your index finger around the edges, and flick your wrist when you release it." Again, he shows me in slow motion. I lower my arm, bending to the side, and plop the stone into the water with one *plop.*

Billy searches the beach and comes back with another stone. "Take it," he says. I take it in my right hand. "Widen your stance," he says. "Like a batter at the plate." I follow his instructions and widen my stance like a batter at the plate. He comes around my backside and takes me, his left arm around my midsection, his right hand holding my right. "Bend down a bit," he says. I bend a bit, and his body follows with me. "Take the stone back," he says. I take the stone back, at shoulder height.

"No," he says and, with his hand on my wrist, lowers my hand to waist level.

I can almost feel the bare skin of his chest on my back through my shirt. His right hand is firmly on my right wrist. His breath is warm on the back of my neck. He pulls my right hand back, still at waist level. He eases his grip on my arm. "Release," he says softly into my right ear. His arm is free as I fling the stone, and I count the skips until they pass ten.

You can swim if you want to, but I wouldn't recommend it. The lake-bottom is rocky, and the water is cold enough to shrivel your privates. We walk along the shoreline until we come to a clearing by the shore. One hop up and we are in what might be called a small meadow. It's really only a small clearing, but I'm in a meadow frame of mind.

We sit down on the grass and look back out on the lake. The sun is warm on our bodies. There are a couple of butterflies wafting about. I point to them, and Billy turns his head and smiles. I fall on my back and look up at Billy. "Do I know you well enough now to ask you what it is like to be half this and half that?" I ask.

Billy laughs. "Do I know you well enough to tell you?"

I smile. "We share a tent," I say. "We can share some thoughts."

Billy looks out to the lake. "All I know is who I am," he says. "Just like you."

Boy, that one spiked. If he only knew. That's how I had the balls to ask him such a personal question in the first place.

"Yeah," I say. "Just like me."

Billy picks at a blade of grass. "What do you want to know?" he asks.

"Well," I start. "You're half, what, Dakota and half white? Do you favor one over the other?"

"No," Billy says. "I'm just me. I am this and I am that, but in the end, I'm just me."

"Well, tell me about this and then tell me about that and then tell me about me."

Billy shrugs. "Okay," he says. "As I told you, my father was Dakota and my mother is white. My father died right after I was born, and my mother raised me. But she made sure that I was aware of my Native American side, so I spent summers with my father's brother, Red Eagle, on the reservation."

"Yeah, you already told me that. What's it like on the

reservation? What did you learn that you wouldn't have learned elsewhere?"

"Well, reservations are like a small town. Mostly they were trailers, but there could be a house or two. At least, when I was growing up. When I was growing up, the casinos were not what they are now. Before, the people were pretty poor, but now, some of the reservations have a lot of money because of the casinos. But some are still pretty poor."

"Did your uncle have a house?"

"Yeah, he had a house. There were a couple of teepees, but they were just ceremonial."

"What else?"

"There is a sweat lodge."

"Sweat lodge. I've heard something about them."

"In the old days, sweat lodges were just blankets or animal hides thrown over cut tree saplings. A fire was built, and large rocks were put in the fire. When they were hot enough, they were brought into the sweat lodge, usually brought by placing two saplings or tree branches beneath and on either side of the rock and bringing it in like a wheelless wheelbarrow. I've heard that sometimes they just kicked them into the middle of the lodge. But that doesn't matter. It's what goes on when they are in the lodge."

"What's that?"

"Well, I haven't been in too many, but I understand it can get quite mystical."

"But you have been in one?"

"Yeah," says Billy. "It's like a sauna, only dark. It takes a while for your eyes to get used to it. You sweat and you talk. And somehow you feel a little closer to the Great Spirit Wakan Tanka."

"So Wakan, ah, Tonk ..."

"Wakan Tanka," Billy corrects.

"Yeah, Wakan Tanka is your god."

"Well, yeah, I guess you could call him that," says Billy. "He did create the world. But he is more than that. He is the Great Spirit. And I think we think of him more as a spirit than God, at least in the traditional sense."

"How do you mean?"

"In the Western world, all the gods are separate—they stand apart from man. The Christian God lives in heaven, separate from the earth. Same thing with Islam. Allah is up there, and if you follow his laws, you can join him in paradise when you die. Go back in time—Apollo lived on Mount Olympus. Odin lived in Asgard. All of these gods were separated from the people who believed in them, and one could only be with them after death. But we believe that Wakan Tanka is with us on this earth. He is the Great Spirit that flows through the trees and the rivers and the plains. He touches everything. And he is here now. He shows the way here on earth."

"Interesting," I say.

"He—I'm using the term *he* here, but I could just as well say *it*. Doesn't really matter. It is more like the eastern religions. Not so much Hindu, with their multiplicity of gods, or the Japanese Shinto ancestor worship. It is more like Buddhism or Taoism. But I believe those two religions were formed long after Asians crossed the Bering Strait during the last Ice Age. So perhaps there was something earlier that the émigrés took with them that somehow, later, influenced Gautama and Lao Tzu and, perhaps, Confucius."

"Interesting. I hadn't thought of that."

"Nobody really knows. But with Native American religions, there is a distinction from the Western religions and a similarity with the Eastern religions, or should I say, philosophies. The Eastern religions are more of a philosophy than the fire-breathing rectifiers of the Western world."

"So ... the Great Spirit is here now."

"Definitely. If you follow Wakan Tanka, take only what you need, and put back what you don't use, the grass will grow and the rivers will run clean. You will have all that you need. The main difference is that the Spirit is here, not in some far-off place."

I nod my head in contemplation.

"That is an over simplification. But I hope you understand."

I reach down and caress the ground, pointing to a single blade of grass. "Is the spirit in this little blade of grass?"

"Yes," says Billy.

"And that?" I say, pointing to the nearest pine.

Billy smiles and nods.

I lie down on my back, the sun warming my body. I close my eyes and try to feel it. I smell the fresh pine and feel the breeze that has just flowed across a clear blue mountain lake. And I understand what it is to be alive.

I'm lying on my back in the meadow grass. My eyes are closed as I feel the heat of the sun on my face. I feel Billy pass his hand over me, caressing my hair back from my forehead. I open my eyes. Billy is sitting cross-legged, each hand on a knee, eyes closed, head uplifted to fully catch the sun. I blink. "Billy," I say. "Did you just, ah, just touch me?"

Billy keeps his head up and eyes closed. "No," he says. "You probably just felt the wind."

"Huh ..." I think out loud. "I thought for sure ..."

"The wind," Billy says. "It can play tricks on you in the mountains."

"I s'pose," I say and close my eyes again and drift off.

I feel a hand lightly caressing my body, from my chest to my stomach. I open my eyes. Billy is still sitting cross-legged, a hand on each knee, eyes closed, head uplifted as if in a trance.

I lift myself up on my right elbow. I open my mouth to say something, but nothing comes out. I close my mouth and lower myself down on my back again. And close my eyes once more.

I open my eyes. Next to me, Billy is still sitting cross-legged, hands on knees, head uplifted to the sun. What a magnificent creature, black hair flowing to his shoulders, chiseled arms and chest. He seems so at ease with himself. Just a single soul set free. So sure of himself. I want to be like that. I want to be free. I want to know myself. And I want to like what I know. Billy opens his eyes.

"Welcome back," I say to Billy.

Billy smiles.

"You were praying to the Great Spirit?"

Billy shrugs. "I s'pose you might say that."

"How do I—"

Billy stops me. "You don't pray to Wakan Tanka. That is the difference between the two cultures. In his *Devil's Dictionary*, Ambrose Bierce defines prayer as 'to ask that the laws of the universe be annulled in behalf of a single petitioner, confessedly unworthy.' The white man always wants to have nature change for his benefit. In the Native American culture, we acknowledge nature and try to become natural, become part of nature and act within nature's rules. You'd be surprised what is there, once you tap in."

"But how do you ..."

"You just acknowledge it. Relax and let it happen."

"Would it feel like, ah, like a hand softly caressing you?"

Billy turns his head to me, and smiles.

"Let's take a walk," says Billy. "There's a trail that goes by the shore, around the lake."

We get up and leave our little garden. The trail is bumpy with rocks protruding, but it has a good view of the lake. Just watch your step.

"Tell me some more about Wakan Tanka," I say.

"What do you want to know?" asks Billy.

"I don't know ... like, can I touch him?"

Billy steps over a big rock. "It's more like him touching you," he says.

Billy offers me his hand, and I conquer the same rock, but step to the side on the grass. "Wakan Tanka is everywhere," says Billy. "He is in the land and the sky and the trees and the rivers. He is in this lake. He is in the grass under your feet."

"You mean nature, then," I say.

"Well, yeah, you might put it that way," says Billy. "But he is not nature. Nature is there. But just there. You can't commune with nature. It can make you feel good, of course. But Wakan Tanka is more like the caretaker of nature. He presides over it. And in doing so, you might say he presides over us. If we take care of his realm, if we understand that there is something more than making money or creating monuments, then the grass will grow and the rivers will run clean and the flowers will bloom. It is all a matter of believing and acting on your beliefs."

"So, if I believe, and keep his, how should I put it ... if I keep his laws, he may touch me?"

Billy steps over another rock and, without turning his head, says, "I think he already has."

Chapter 16

I WISH I COULD HEAR SOME SNORING. I'M IN BIG BLUE, lying on my side of the tent. Billy is lying in his sleeping bag on his side to the tent. There is ample space between us. But I want to hear snoring. I want to hear the rhythmic cadence of breath confirming that he is gone for the night. I do not want to hear his body roll over and feel his hand on my shoulder. It's not that I wouldn't like it. It's just that I'm not ready for it. I'm not ready to feel his hand on my shoulder pulling me toward him, turning me over, and feel his lips on mine, his hot breath on my neck.

Snoring, I need to hear snoring. I know I am not ready for anything. I don't know what I would do. When it comes, if it comes, I want to be ready. I want to know exactly what to do. I want to be in charge. I want to be in charge of letting go. I want to be in charge of giving myself. It will be my decision. My choice. And it will be what I want.

But for now, I would like to hear that smooth rattle of breath from across the tent that tells me I am safe. For now.

Where am I? I'm at my father's house, where I grew up. I'm in my walk-in closet getting ready for bed. I have taken my shorts off and folded them neatly before placing them on the shelf. I turn. Billy is by the closet door.

A low moan wakens me. I am in my sleeping bag. In Big Blue. Billy is across from me, in his, still asleep. An ample space separates us. I uncurl my toes and wipe the perspiration that has formed on my upper lip. One more look at Billy in his sleeping bag. I turn to look up at the top of Big Blue and let out a muffled laugh. Then I turn to the side, away from Billy, and try to make sense of the images and thoughts racing through my head.

Big Blue, you gotta help me here. What's with me being in my father's house? I know I grew up there, and Lisa says I can stay there until it sells, although I should really move out. Then it would be really clean and ready for a buyer. I only have my bedroom and a dinette in the kitchen. I try to keep it as clean as a twenty-one-year-old can.

Do I have an Electra complex? I know I loved my dad. But I didn't *love* my dad. I know my mother did. And I am my mother. So my mother loved him. I am my mother. So I loved him. That's a syllogism. But it's a silly syllogism. I know my feelings. And what about Billy? Why was he there? Do I have some hidden desire here? Maybe. I could do worse. I mean, he is good-looking. And he is intelligent. And he has a free spirit about him. I like being with him. And he has long black hair. Do I have some hidden desire? *Big Blue, you're going to have to help me out with this one.*

Sunlight is shining on the tent. Boy, I must have slept in this morning. In the mountains, not only does the sun have to come up—it has to get over the mountains to shine on you. I don't remember sleeping this long. It must be the mountain air. Or maybe I'm just relaxed. Or maybe I was too tired. Or maybe I was afraid to wake up. Anyway, I'm awake now. I look over at Billy's sleeping bag. It is lying, unburdened, on the tent floor. Billy must be up and about. I quickly get dressed and walk out of the tent. Billy is sitting cross-legged in front of the tent. He has some sort of stick, like a sawn-off branch, in his left hand and another branch in his right hand. It's big. He is pounding it against the sides of the stick in his left hand, using it like a hammer.

"Whatcha doin'?" I ask.

Billy holds out the branch. "What do you see?" he asks.

"A branch," I say.

"What else?"

"I don't know. Wood, bark ..."

"Yes," says Billy. "It is a branch. But what can it become?"

I think for a minute. "Firewood or maybe kindling for a fire."

"What else?"

"Ah, maybe ... a stake. You could whittle it down and it could be a stake."

"Yes, it could be a stake. What else?"

I think for another minute. "I don't know, Billy. What can it become?"

Billy twirls it slowly around his hand while looking at it. "When a man sees this, he sees only a branch. But when a wise man holds it, he looks inside it and sees what it can become."

"And what do you see when you look inside that branch?"

Billy starts banging on the stick again. "A flute," he says.

I'm not wearing a bra this morning. I don't know—I just feel freer. And after the dream last night, I just—I don't know—I just feel freer. Besides, I'm going down to the lake to wash my pits. It's been a couple of days. I will hike the path around the lake until I know no one is coming, and it will be much easier to just whip off my T-shirt. If someone does come along, I don't want to wrangle with my bra and then try to pull my shirt over it. Just a quick off and quick on.

I've walked the path for a while and am sure no one else is coming. At least for a while. I take off my tennis shoes and socks, take one more look down the trail, and pull my T-shirt off. I dip my toes in. Then I take a big step and I'm into the lake up to my knees. Jeez, it's cold. I have a bar of soap in a plastic soap dish. I splash water on my pits, soap up, rinse off, splash my face for good measure, and hop out of the water in record time. A quick toweling off and my T-shirt is back on, no one the wiser. I sit along the bank. The sun is already hot on my skin. I lean back on the grass, feel the heat, and close my eyes. My mind goes back to my dream. Billy is holding me tightly to him. His mouth is on mine. He lays me down on the closet floor.

As I approach the campsite, Billy is examining what looks like a tree branch.

"Are you really going to make a flute out of that tree branch?" I ask as I get closer.

Billy looks up. "It's not a tree branch," he says. "It is sumac. I found this piece when I was in South Dakota. Sumac does not grow at this altitude."

"Why sumac?" I ask.

Billy rubs his chin. "What I want to do is to make a Native American flute, but only using what Native Americans had years ago. I will assume that they had some kind of knife. But I'm not going to just get a sharp stone. A metal knife is all that I have that is man-made."

"Using only a sharp stone would be impossible," I offer.

"No, not impossible," says Billy. "But I don't have the time to find out how long that would take. So a knife will do. A knife, a piece of deer antler, a stone, leather straps, and some tree sap."

"Deer antler?"

"Just a piece. I'll show you in a minute. This may take a while, so if you have something else you would like to do ..."

"No, no," I say enthusiastically. "I'd really like to watch. So why were you pounding on the wood for so long?"

"I will have to cut off the bark after I put this together, and banging the other branch against it will loosen it up and make it easier to cut the bark off."

"Tree sap?" I query.

"Later," says Billy. "First, I have to split this wood."

Billy gets up on his knees, puts the wood on end, perpendicular, and places the knife on the top. He picks up a large rock, steadies the knife, and with a few whacks, pounds the knife down the center of the wood a few inches. Billy puts his fingers in the gap, the wood splits, and he pulls the sides apart.

"There," says Billy. "Once you get the knife started properly, the wood will pull apart. It will follow its natural grain. This wood is only about two feet in length, so it was an easy split."

"How did you determine the length?" I ask.

"When Native Americans first started making flutes, they didn't have tape measures and such. They usually used distances between parts of the body. Some flutes are the length from your armpit to your wrists. Others may be from your elbow to the end of your fingers. If you use some measurement that has to do with your body, it is more natural. This one," he says, holding it up to eye level, "is from my elbow to my fingertips. If this turns out like I think it will, I want to carry it around with me. And I need it to fit into my backpack."

Billy puts one side of the wood down and turns the other side to me. "See this sort of yellow-brown streak?" he asks.

I nod.

"This is the pith of the plant. And it is soft and easy to clean out. That is why I picked sumac. Probably the best flutes are made of hard wood, like red cedar. But with really hard wood, you would need machines. You would need a band saw, a drill, sandpaper, and stuff. I wanted to do this like my forefathers did. It will take a bit longer, and the flute will probably not be so melodic, but this is what I want to do."

"I definitely want to watch this now," I say.

Billy takes the one strip of wood in his left hand and picks up a piece of antler. "Normally, you would use a hook saw for this," says Billy.

"A hook saw?"

"Yeah, it is usually used for cleaning hooves of horses. But before I start on the inside, I want to take the bark off the outside." Billy picks up the other piece and puts them together. He eyeballs it to make sure the ends are together and the split sides are held in place. He picks up a strap of leather and puts one end in his mouth, and the other he wraps around the wood. When the strap is tight around the wood, he drops the leather from his mouth and ties it tight against the wood.

"Before I take the bark off, I have to mark the plug," he says.

"The plug?" I ask.

"Some people call it a wall; others call it a plug. I am going to hollow out the inside of this branch, but there has to be a plug or a wall inside."

Using his knife as a guide, he says, "Air will be blown in from this end, hit the plug, and be forced up and over to the other side. The other side will have a hole on top, right after the plug, and a hollow end extending to the remaining length of the flute. Finger holes will be in this end to vary the pitch."

Billy takes the knife and cuts the circumference of the branch. Then he makes another cut around the branch, about a thumb-space apart. "Now," he says. "I have measured the plug width and can start taking the rest of the bark off."

He puts the knife to the wood, and the bark on either side of the plug space is quickly off. "I'll scrape down this end to narrow the mouthpiece," he says. The knife works the wood until the end is tapered. Untying the leather strap, he separates the two pieces. "Now we can start hollowing out the flute," he says. He makes a cut on either side of the plug and then down the length of the wood. "I can loosen the wood with the knife," he says. "But it would be very difficult to hollow out with just the knife. But see how the antler's tip is bent?" He brings the antler up to eye level. "This is perfect for digging it out. You cut the wood lengthwise with the knife, but you dig it out widthwise with the curved tip of the antler."

"You gotta be kiddin'," I say.

Billy throws me a glance.

"Where did you get the antler?" I ask.

"It's from my first kill," answers Billy.

"I'd like to hear about it," I say.

Billy shakes his head. "Maybe later."

Billy just keeps working away, and soon both pieces of wood are hollowed out on either side of the plug.

"I have left this strip of bark on the wood to mark where the plug will be," says Billy. "Now we have to make two holes, one on either side of the plug."

Billy takes his knife point to the wood, and with effort, two holes appear on either side of the plug. "Now, these are holes," says Billy, "but they really should be square because the air will be flowing over them. It would be easier to have an X-Acto knife, but this knife will have to do."

Billy works both holes and gets them remarkably square. "Now, the plug is just below the space between the holes. We have to shave the wood down to where there will be a passageway for the air in front of the plug to go up and over the plug and into the sound chamber. But first, I have to shave the hole behind the plug and give it sort of an angle to split the air that comes through. Some air will go up and out of the flute, but most of the air will be directed to the sound chamber." Some more digging, and Billy says, "Now we do the finger holes."

Billy puts his hand on the flute, just behind the second hole. Spreading his fingers, he says, "This will be the first hole." He makes an indentation in the wood with his knife point. He puts his thumb next to the indentation and puts his knife to the other side of his thumb. "There has to be the same distance between holes to have an accurate melodic sound, so these holes will be a thumb-width apart," he says, and quickly five holes are in the wood. Billy blows the sawdust off and out of the wood.

He brings up the other side of the split wood, places them together, and examines them. "Good fit," he says. "Now for some tree sap."

"Tree sap?" I ask.

"Yeah," says Billy. "We have to bind these two halves together. My forefathers never had glue. So we'll use tree sap." He gets up. "Yesterday I found a white pine and cut it. White pines bleed easily, and there should be plenty of sap by now."

Billy walks out of the campsite, but is back in a few minutes, holding the two pieces together. He sits down in front of me again. Grabbing a leather strap, he puts one end in his mouth and wraps the other tightly around the flute.

"We could just wrap leather straps around the wood, but there might be some edges that, for some reason, do not quite fit back together. The tree sap will make a good glue and fill any gaps so we have good air flow." Another leather strap is affixed toward the other end.

"I have cut a piece off the long end to make a bird," he says.

"A what?"

"A bird. I have to have a piece of wood to cover the first hole before the plug so the air does not escape upward and out before it reaches the plug. I have cut the piece off the end about an inch and split it in two. The center has been cut out and will follow the natural curve of the flute but will block the air from escaping upward."

With a strip of leather, Billy ties the bird to the top of the flute above the plug. "You don't cement the bird in place because you may want to move it to get a different sound. A lot of people make a design for a decorative bird. Some like to call it a fetish or something else. But I just like the term *bird*."

Billy puts the mouthpiece to his lips and blows. His

fingers are on the finger holes. I lie back in the warm grass. I close my eyes and listen to Billy and the melodic tune coming from the flute. I open my eyes and there is a butterfly traipsing about overhead. It is a beautiful butterfly, one that I have not seen before. It is somewhat stationary, but flutters about. I may be mistaken, but it seems to rise and fall with the changing tones of the flute. Am I dreaming? Is this just my imagination? But it does flutter about. And it is beautiful. I close my eyes and listen to the longing song of the flute. I open my eyes, and the butterfly is gone. I listen to the soft music for a while, feel the warm breeze flow over my body, close my eyes, and drift away.

Chapter 17

I'M LYING ON MY SIDE, MY LEFT HAND EXTENDED UP TO cradle my head. Billy is sitting cross-legged in front of the fire pit. We've finished our dinner, and I'm on my second glass of wine, Billy is nursing his second beer.

"So," I say to Billy. "Tell me about the antler and your first kill."

Billy shrugs and takes a swig. Wiping his wrist across his mouth to catch the foam, he says, "You really want to know?"

"Yes," I say. "I really do. And don't leave anything out just 'cause I'm a girl."

"You want the whole story?" asks Billy.

"Don't leave out a thing," I counter.

"Well, okay," says Billy. "I'll give you the whole story."

I nod and take another sip of wine.

"As I told you," Billy starts, "my mother is white, and my father was Dakota Sioux. They fell in love, and I was born. There not too much opportunity for a Native American, job-wise. The only place where a Native American could get treated equally was the armed forces. There they didn't care about the color of your skin. Just your ability. So my father died when I was young. My mother worked full time, and there were some survivor benefits, so we did okay. But my mother wanted me to know my Native American heritage, so I lived with her for nine months in the winter, going to school, and the summers I would go to the Prairie Island Dakota reservation by Red Wing."

"Yes, I know of that," I interject. "That's where they have a casino."

"Yeah, says Billy. "And a nuclear power plant as well."

I nod.

"Anyway, my uncle, my father's brother, Red Eagle, lived at the reservation, and he let me stay with him in the summers. He would do his best to teach me the Native American ways."

"That's where you learned about the flute," I say.

Billy nods. "And hunting and hand-to-hand combat and some other things."

"Like how to take a feather from an eagle in the wild."

Billy nods. "And other things."

"Like …?"

"We're getting a little off track. Let's save those for another time."

I nod again. "Another time," I say. "Promise?"

"Yeah, we'll see."

"Okay, continue."

"Okay," says Billy after another swig. "When I was about thirteen, Red Eagle said it was time I learned to hunt. I was all ears. I had sat around the campfires and listened to all the stories, and now it was my turn. I was really excited."

"I can imagine."

"Normally, if you go stomping through the woods, you are never going to find a deer. Hunting is only legal in the fall, and the bucks are in the rut. That is their mating season, and their senses are heightened. They can hear you coming from a long ways away. You will never see them. That is why many hunters use a deer stand. Some are on the ground and camouflaged, and others are up in trees, either a platform or a hanging chair attached to a tree. Deer don't look up. There are no natural predators of deer from up above, so their vision is always at ground level, where their natural predators, like the wolf, are. You can be up in a tree stand and they can walk right past you. That is, if they don't hear you breathe or smell you, which they could and would. The key is to find a trail where they are feeding, climb up, and wait for one to come by."

"So, how did you do this?" I ask.

"Red Eagle had scouted a cornfield near the reservation," says Billy. "Deer will often eat the corn that is left on the ground after harvesting. It really fattens them up. Anyway, Red Eagle had found a trail in the forest next to a cornfield that had hoof tracks and deer droppings. So we picked the day, and he took me to the cornfield. When I got out of the car, he told me to take off my clothes. I was kind of shocked. He threw me a plastic bag and told me that he had smoked some of my clothes the night before—placed them over a smoky fire and put them in the plastic bag. As I said before, when the male deer is in the rut, his sense of smell is acute. But the smoky clothes would cloak my scent. After I changed into the smoky clothes, he told me to turn around and lift up my right foot, backward to him. He took out a vial and sprinkled some foul-smelling stuff on the sole of my boot, explaining that when I would be up in the tree, a male deer in the rut could even smell me through the soles of my boots. This foul-smelling substance was fox scent. Actually it was fox urine. And it smelled like it. It certainly would cloak my scent."

"Where do you get fox urine?" I ask.

"Good hunting stores will have it," says Billy. "When I was fixed up, scent-wise, he handed me my bow and arrows. He wanted me to learn how to hunt the way our ancestors hunted, before the white man came. So it was bow-and-arrow time. Fortunately, he had made me practice, and I was a pretty good shot for my age.

"I followed him onto the trail, and shortly we were at a large tree next to the trail. He held my bow and arrows until I was up on the first branch. I found two branches, one about eight feet off the ground for my feet and the other about ten feet off the ground for my butt. So I would be able to sit and wait, the tree sheltering me from the sight of anything coming down the trail from the woods. Red Eagle turned and, without saying a word, was gone.

"I waited for an hour or so," Billy continues. "But now the skies were turning black with rainclouds. I figured that this would be the end of the hunt. Raindrops were falling and making a pattering sound on the ground. Then I heard the crunching of leaves on the trail behind the tree. I put an arrow to the bowstring and froze. Another crunching of leaves, and a deer head appeared the other side of the tree. Then the antlers appeared, then the shoulder of this magnificent animal. Red Eagle had told me to aim for a spot right behind the shoulder of the animal, 'cause that is where the heart is. Normally, you can't bring a large deer down right away with a bow and arrow, unless it is a compound bow, which packs a lot of firepower. Even with a small-to-medium-caliber rifle, it is hard to bring a large deer down right away because they are filled with so much adrenaline and can run on just like that for a while, even with a hole in their heart.

"I drew the string back, held my breath, made sure of my aim, and let it go. I knew I had a good shot when I saw the arrow fletches disappear through a hole just behind the deer's shoulder. The deer bolted around and crashed through the brush and bushes. I jumped down from the tree, slightly spraining my left ankle. I quickly found the blood trail and started to track the animal. There was a

100

good blood trail, and its hooves had made tracks in the ground. More rain, this time heavier. I followed the blood trail a little more, and then it started to pour. The skies opened up, and before long, the blood trail was gone. Even the hoofprints were washed away in the deluge. I fell to my knees and cried like a baby."

"So it was gone?" I ask.

"Yeah, it was gone," he says. "And so was the trail."

Billy doesn't say anything. I wait. He still doesn't say anything.

"So ...?" I ask.

Billy shrugs. "It was gone."

I scrunch my eyebrows. "Now, wait a minute," I say. "You said this was your first kill, and now you say it was gone."

"Well, it *was* gone," answers Billy. "With the blood trail and the hoofprints gone, there was no way to find it."

"I can't believe ..."

"Until Red Eagle found me."

"Why, you ..."

"I'm dry," says Billy, shaking his beer can. He gets up, takes a new can from the cooler, cracks the pop-top. "Ya know that thing they say about Injuns not being able to hold their liquor ..." A wry smile comes over his face. "That's just bullshit." He sits down by the fire again. "Let's see, where was I?"

"You shot the deer, the blood trail was gone, and Red Eagle finds you," I say.

"Yeah, right," Billy says and takes a swig. "After the rain stopped, I was sitting in the mud when Red Eagle came up to me and asked me what happened. I told him that I had shot a deer right behind the shoulder, a kill shot, but the rain washed away the blood and hoofprint trail. He asked me, 'How many points?' I told him at least eight, maybe ten—I was so nervous. He said that an eight- or ten-point buck, well fed, would weigh two hundred to maybe two hundred fifty pounds. And if it was running scared, its sharp hooves would make quite a mark in the ground. I told him that it had rained so hard that it washed away all the blood and tracks. He said, 'Not all, if you know where to look.' He said that this was late fall and there were a lot of leaves on the ground. He picked up a small tree branch and swished at a pile of leaves on the ground. He said that the hooves would make an indentation through the leaves and the covering leaves would prevent the rain from washing away the hoofprint. All you have to do is uncover the leaves that hide the hoofprints.

"He handed me another small branch, and we swished away some leaves, and sure enough, there were the hoofprints. More swishes and more uncovered hoofprints. We were able to follow the trail for quite a while, and soon we came upon a stand of sumac. Red Eagle put his hand up. We stopped. I could hear the sound of rasping, as if someone or something was choking. We slowly made our way around the sumac, and there, in an opening, was the deer. Bloody foam was spilling out of its mouth, and its eyes were glazed. Half an arrow, point first, was sticking out of its side. It lowered its head and then raised it, spitting out more bloody foam. Red Eagle signaled to me to put another arrow in it. I put another arrow to the string and pulled back. It seemed as if the deer's eyes blazed through the glaze, and the arrow found its mark, the deer leaped high and then sort of collapsed in midair, tumbling to the ground. Red Eagle quickly ran to it and slit its throat. But I could see it was dead already. Red Eagle found a stick about three feet in length and tied each rear leg of the deer to the ends of the stick, opening the abdomen to full view. He slit the abdomen open, reached in, and cut the trachea and esophagus and heart. At the other end, he cut out the anus, and with a little pull, the intestines just flowed out. He took out three plastic bags and put the heart and kidneys in the first two, and then he held the liver up to me. I know the movies show Indians taking a bite out of the liver of their first kill, but they don't do that anymore. There can be liver flukes, and just drinking its blood is enough. I took the liver, put it to my mouth, and tasted the warm blood, letting some trickle down my chin. Red Eagle said, 'Tonight, the children will have fresh meat.' He raised his arms to the sky and let out a war whoop.

"I put the liver in the plastic bag. Red Eagle went to the head of the deer and cut off a piece of antler. He threw it to me and said, 'You take good care of that. You're going to need it when I show you how to make a flute.'"

Chapter 18

I'M LYING IN MY SLEEPING BAG IN BIG BLUE WITH BILLY AN appropriate distance away. I'm thinking of the day and the night with Billy. A warm glow flows through my body. It's probably the wine. I might have taken a glass too many tonight. I might have ... *Whoa, what is that?* A shimmer just went through my body. A shimmer or some kind of shake. It was as if every molecule in my body was torn apart and put back together in a millisecond. I'm okay. But wow. What *was* that? Probably just the wine.

There is a slight snore coming from across the tent. Yesterday, I wanted to hear a snore. I needed to hear a snore. Tonight? Well, I do have this warm feeling flowing through my body. It may be the wine. But then again, it may not.

I feel a little different this morning. Maybe I'm just hungover. Probably too much wine. Or maybe it's the altitude. We're pretty high up here. I'm just a plains girl. That's probably it. I'll have a little breakfast and be fit as a fiddle. I've got some freeze-dried porridge with strawberries. I'll throw that in a pot of boiling water and be fit as a fiddle. I just hope I have enough propane in the bottle.

Nope, out of propane. I started a campfire with matches. I can do that. And I was going to put a pot of water on the fire to cook the porridge. I knew that the bottom of the pot would get all filthy with soot and such, but I was hungry and in a hurry. We're quite a ways from any store, and I was willing to scrub the bottom of the pot with whatever—for hours, if it took that much time. But Billy saw what I was doing and told me to put some liquid soap around the outside bottom and sides of the pot. He said that when the pot is put on the fire, the smoke and soot will just cling to the soap and it will rinse off with just plain water. No scrubbing. So I put liquid soap around the outsides of the pot, put it on the fire, ate my delicious porridge and strawberries, and headed for the lake. I took a washrag with me just for luck. Son of a beehive, even in the cold mountain water, with just a couple of swishes, the pot was like new. No scrubbing for hours, just a couple of swishes with the washcloth. I'm sure those serious campers, the ones with backpacks, probably know this trick. But I didn't. So I wonder what this magic man has up his sleeve next.

I am back at our campsite. Billy is sitting outside the tent. His sleeping bag is in its sheath, and he is leaning against his rucksack behind him. He is sitting cross-legged, bare-chested, eyes closed, head uplifted to the sun. In his right hand is his eagle feather. Did I mention he has abs?

I wait for a few minutes, as I do not want to interrupt his meditation. After a few minutes, I can wait no longer.

"Thanks for the tip, Billy," I say as I put the clean pot back in my big bag.

Billy shrugs his shoulders. "No problem," he says, eyes still closed.

"Going somewhere?" I ask, somewhat hesitantly.

"I thought it would be nice to go down to Lake McDonald," says Billy.

"And I thought it would be nice if you would tell me how you got that eagle feather," I say.

Billy does not say anything for one minute. With his eyes still closed and his head still uplifted to the sun, he says, "Okay, I'll tell you if you'll take me to Lake McDonald."

Lake McDonald is on the west side of Glacier Park. It is long and beautiful. Billy had originally wanted to camp out at Fish Creek by the lake, bypassing Apgar campground, the second-largest campground in Glacier Park. The west side does not get as much traffic as the east side, I suppose, because there are a lot of people from out east who come to the mountain, find a nice place by a glacier, and camp out for a week or so. And there are a lot of campers and trailers. There are also some sites for tents, but Billy figured that Fish Creek would be better suited for us.

But when we got to Fish Creek campground, the ranger told us that there is a bear trap near the back of the campground. There is a grizzly bear that went a little wilder than they like, and they are trying to trap it and reposition it in a more remote area. Or kill it if they have to. The ranger explained that the grizzly was getting too close to the campground, to people. The ranger advised us not to camp there, and if we found a spot, there would be no food allowed. I almost asked if they considered Chardonnay a food. But I thought better of it and decided to head back to Apgar campground. But I turned to the ranger. "Why don't you use a dart gun or something—or just kill it?"

The expression on the ranger's face went to "This lady doesn't know what she's talking about" but quickly regained its composure. He said, "Sometimes you can capture a wild thing, and sometimes it just goes away."

As we turned the car around, the ranger said in a loud voice, "Sometimes it's best to just let it go."

There certainly are a lot of campers and trailers in Apgar, but another ranger gave us directions to a more secluded site, not far from Lake McDonald. There also is a ministore there where we could stock up on propane and freeze-dried food. So, we're back in the food business. That is, if you call freeze-dried a food.

But the campsite is perfect for us. In this large campground, it is almost like we are by ourselves—which, I guess, we are. We pitch Big Blue in no time and put our gear inside. We walk to the road and follow some other campers down a trail that leads to the lake. It is beautiful. Billy picks up a couple of stones and skips them across the water, counting the skips. I try to get to two.

Billy points to an eagle sitting on a tree branch down the beach. "That eagle is getting ready to hunt," he says. "And when he takes off, he will head south, flapping his wings to gain altitude and then turn back to the north to soar."

"How do you know that?" I ask.

"Look at the waves," he says. "Not by the shore, but

out in the bay. The waves are heading south, which means the wind is from the north. Eagles will try to soar into the wind if they are over water. In the summer, the trees in the forest will absorb heat from the sun. Sometimes that heat will rise and create updrafts called thermals. When an eagle finds a thermal over land, it can hang around indefinitely, going in any direction. But over water, there are no updrafts. They can flap their wings to gain altitude and fly in different directions, but they need to fly into the wind to soar. And when I use the term *soar*, I just mean to maintain altitude without having to flap their wings."

"Ah, I'm not sure I understand," I say.

"An eagle's wing, and actually any flying bird's wing, is convex on top and concave beneath. It is like an airplane wing. This curvature will give it lift. It is called Bernoulli's principle. The air going over the top of the wing is stretched out and becomes thinner, while the air flowing under the wing is compressed and becomes thick. This imbalance of air pressure sort of pushes the wing upward, giving it what we call lift. So an eagle can soar for some distance without flapping its wings when it is heading into the wind. But has to flap its wings when going with the wind. It may look like an eagle is soaring when it is flying with the wind, but it has to lose altitude to have enough speed to force air over its wings. This is quite an oversimplification, but it works. There are some variations going into the wind at an angle, but I won't take up your time with that."

I just smile and try to shake my head without him noticing.

"Now, if an eagle starts out over water with the wind behind him," Billy continues, "you'll notice that he will make somewhat of a thin semicircle. And when he turns back, he will take more of a straight line to take advantage of the wind direction. That is, if he thinks there is good hunting there. So the route will be something like a large thin *D* in the sky, with an arc to gain altitude and then a somewhat straight line for soaring into the wind. If you watch long enough, you'll see a pattern."

"But why wouldn't it just make a straight line to where it would turn around?" I say. "Wouldn't it get there sooner?"

"Yes, it would," answers Billy. "And sometimes they do. But then it would be going over the same territory twice. Making an arc would give them an extra chance to catch sight of something."

"Then why wouldn't it just go around in circles to expand its search?" I ask.

"Well," says Billy, "as any hunter knows, you can find and track prey better when your body parts are still. You don't see hunters flailing their arms about while searching for prey. You'd just scare them off. It's better that they don't know you're coming."

Billy picks up another stone and makes another toss.

"What's the prettiest place you have been?" I ask.

Billy's stone skips across the water. I stop counting at ten as it dribbles into the water. "All the Rockies are great," he says. "From Colorado to Idaho and Montana. But if I had to choose one place, it would be in Alberta. Banff and Lake Louise and Lake Moraine. And oh, yes, can't forget Emerald Lake. It would be tough to choose between those. But they are relatively close to each other, just west of Calgary. They are unmatched by anything I've seen in the States." Billy points to the sky. "See that eagle?" he says. "If that eagle heads north, it could be there in, oh, about ten hours. If it had the stamina—which it doesn't."

I watch the eagle for a while and wonder what it would be like to be free, to be clean, to just float around in the air, to be one with nature, to be ... normal. And I wonder if I have the stamina, the stamina to go to a beautiful place, the stamina to live my life to the fullest, the stamina to take me to a natural end.

We walk along the lakeshore for a while, and I almost feel like reaching out and taking his hand. I don't. We're just campers, right? Just two lost souls sharing some time together. Sharing some time in one of the most beautiful places on the continent. Sharing some time. But where will this thing go? I must say—I'm just starting to get some feelings. Well, just starting might not be the most correct way of putting it. I watch as Billy flings some stones into the lake and makes them skip countless times. And I like how his long black hair wafts about his head with each fling and comes back in perfect place afterward, daring him to make another toss. There is an air about him that tells you that he knows things that you don't know, but that he would rather keep to himself. And I want to know more about him. And I wonder if he already knows that.

I hope the Chardonnay is cold. I'm going to need some tonight.

We're sitting around the campfire that Billy has skillfully built—one match, no paper. I suppose I could have asked him to build it sans match, but we'll save that for another time. I am on the last sip of my first glass of Chardonnay. Billy has finished his first beer and heads for the cooler.

"I think we were talking about the eagle," I say.

Billy takes a cool one from the cooler, comes back to the fire, and sits down, cross-legged.

"The eagle," he says.

"Yes," I say. "The eagle and the eagle feather."

Billy cracks open the beer. "Well, what do you want to know?"

I take my last swig as the wine empties the glass. It swirls in my mouth before I swallow. I'm starting to feel the warm glow of the elixir. "Everything," I say.

"Well, then you might want to get a refill," says Billy.

I get to my feet, refill my glass from the bottle in the cooler, and sit back down, cross-legged, trying to imitate Billy.

Billy takes a swig from the can. "We believe that every living thing has a spirit. Some might think it is energy flowing through it. The Chinese call it *chi*. That term is derived from the Taoist religion. By the way, that is the fundamental idea behind acupuncture. They believe that there are meridians in your body that allow the chi to flow. When a meridian is blocked, the chi, or energy, cannot flow freely, and the needle will open up the meridian and allow the chi to flow freely. The Native American philosophy is not as specific as that. We just believe that in every living thing is a spirit. It is not a ghost or anything like that. You might think of it as energy specific to that individual or species, but we believe that every living thing has some type of energy. And we call that *spirit*.

"There is a theory that during the last Ice Age a land or ice bridge developed over what is now the Bering Strait and people from Asia passed over and migrated onto and populated this continent. It is possible that we share a common ancestor and—"

"The eagle feather, Billy. You were talking about the eagle feather."

Billy turns to me and says, "Good madam, stay awhile; I will be faithful."

"What was that?" I ask.

"That was Polonius talking to Gertrude, Hamlet's mother."

I laugh. "Of course it was. So you know Shakespeare."

"Just enough to get me into trouble."

I laugh again. "Continue."

"What I'm getting at," says Billy, "is that all living things have an energy. You may call it chi, or spirit, or whatever. And there can be a connection between living things. If you just pick up a feather off the ground, there will be no spirit in that feather. If you kill an eagle and then take its feathers, there is no spirit in the bird or the feather. But if you can take a feather from a living eagle in the wild, well, I believe you can capture some of its spirit. You will have a connection."

"Our first night together, when we asked to camp out on Chief's land," I say. "Is that why Chief asked you, 'Does the eagle still fly?'"

"Yes," says Billy.

"And when you answered, 'It still flies,' he knew, and that is why he smiled."

Billy nods. "He knew."

"Cool," I say and take another sip of wine. "Now I'm ready to hear how you take a feather from a live eagle in the wild."

Billy closes his eyes for a moment and takes a couple of breaths. He opens his eyes and looks to the sky and then into the campfire.

"In Sun Tzu's book, *The Art of War*, he says that all battles are won or lost before they are fought. It is in the preparation. You must understand your enemy." He takes a swig of beer and lets it settle before going on. "I spent a lot of time in northern Wisconsin," he continues. "There are quite a few eagles up there. On one camping trip, I saw an eagle's nest up in a tall tree. From a hiding spot, I watched how the eagle would leave and come back to the nest. Usually it would hunt for fish, but eagles are birds of opportunity. It will even take a small dog if it can. I would come back to the spot for a few days and take note of when it would leave the nest and when it came back, which direction it went, and from which direction it came back. There was a clearing in the forest that it would fly over. There were tall pines, but there also were plenty of oaks and maples, deciduous trees."

"De ... what?" I manage.

"Trees that lose their leaves in the fall," Billy answers. "This would be a good place. I made a very large pile of leaves near the middle of the clearing and waited for a few days, so the eagle would get used to having the pile of leaves just lying there. For a few days before I planned the taking, I would bury myself under the leaf pile, leaving only an opening for one eye. For the next few days, I watched the eagle fly over and took note of any changes in his route or demeanor. A few days before, I had trapped a rabbit and kept it alive. When I figured that it would be a good day for the hunt, I went out to the clearing quite a bit earlier than normal. I had picked a calm day so the wind would not be a factor. I put a stake in the ground, tied a rope to the rabbit's rear leg, and tied the rope to the stake. I got under the leaf pile next to the rabbit, positioning myself to face north."

"Why face north?" I ask.

"Well," continues Billy, "eagles are very smart hunters, with very keen eyesight. I figured that the eagle would see the rabbit, circle for a while, and come in from the north."

"Why would the eagle come in from the north?" I ask. "What's the difference?"

Billy shrugs. "Because, as I said, eagles are very smart hunters. They know that if the prey knows they are coming, the prey will skitter away. I was at about forty-five degrees north latitude. The sun is in the south. If the eagle were to come in from the south, the prey would see the eagle's shadow as it descended and try to run away. But if it came in from the north, its shadow would be cast behind it as it swooped down for the kill."

"Jeez," I say and choke out a laugh.

"So, I waited and waited, and finally, I saw the eagle circling above. I knew it would come in for the kill, and sure enough, it swooped down. When its claws dug into the rabbit's flesh, it started to climb, but the rope held, and with the eagle's talons stuck in the rabbit, the eagle tumbled. I crashed my hand down on the eagle, probably stunning it momentarily. I rolled from the leaf pile and had it in my hands."

"Oh my," I manage to say through the hand that has come to cover my mouth.

"It was hacking the hell out of my arms and hands, as you can imagine," continues Billy. "Then it was just a matter of lowering the eagle and then throwing it into the air. The eagle screeched as it flew up and around the trees and was gone. I looked down at my bloody arms to an eagle feather in my hand."

"Jeez," I manage. "What did you do then?"

"With the feather in my hand, I raised my bloody arms to the sky and let out a war whoop."

"How badly were you cut up?" I ask.

"I had covered my hands and arms with leather strapping, so they weren't cut too bad. Look." Billy holds his arms out to me. "See," he says, pointing to scars. "These are from the eagle."

I point to scars farther up on his left arm. "And these too?" I ask.

"No. Those are from an egret," says Billy.

"An egret?" I ask.

"Another story," he says. "But the main thing is that I

have this feather." He pulls his eagle feather from behind him and holds it up to me. "This is my eagle feather, and I believe that the eagle I took it from and I are somehow connected. When I meditate in the sun and lift my head to the sky, I can feel something. It is a feeling that I had never had before. But it is there."

I am lying in my sleeping bag thinking of the day, thinking of Billy and what he has done. And what he can do. Billy is sitting cross-legged on his sleeping bag, fingering what, a few hours ago, was a tree branch and now is a flute.

"Do you mind if I play the flute for a while before bed?" he asks.

Half laughing, I say, "No, Billy, go right ahead."

Billy puts the flute to his mouth, and a haunting, breathless sound fills the tent.

I think about Billy. I think about the chiseled chest and long black hair. I think about making a flute out of a tree branch. I think about hunting a deer and tracking it even though the rain has washed away the tracks. I think about taking an eagle feather from a live eagle in the wild.

I close my eyes and listen to the melodic tones. It is almost as if it were calling me. Is this the sirens' song? Is this what Odysseus heard when he was strapped to the mast, screaming to his oarsmen to pull toward the shore? If I continue to listen, will I be pulled to the shore and crashed against the rocks? I don't care. I unzip my sleeping bag. Raising my hips, I slide my panties down and off. I raise myself up and on my knees. In two knee-steps I am next to Billy. I pull my T-shirt up and off and throw it on the tent floor. Billy is still playing the melodic, mesmerizing tones. I reach down and put my soft hand on his warm shoulder.

Chapter 19

I AM AWAKE. MY SLEEPING BAG IS WET WITH PERSPIRATION. I have a splitting headache. My mouth is dry. But I think back to last night, a night that I have never experienced before. With my eyes closed, I reach out to touch Billy. My hand only finds the emptiness of the nylon floor of Big Blue. I scrunch over a bit and extend my hand again. More nylon. I open my eyes. Billy's side of Big Blue is empty. I hold my breath and listen for the crunch of boot against twig outside. Perhaps Billy has rolled up his sleeping bag and brought his rucksack outside the tent. Maybe he has hiked down to the latrine. He'll be back shortly. And I wonder where he will take me next.

Where's my Billy? He's been gone all day. Did he leave me? I don't know. I'm starting to wonder. I went to the ranger station and paid for another night at the campsite. I can't just leave now. I wouldn't know where to go anyway. That Billy Boy is going to get a talking-to when he gets back.

I've been watching an eagle. I think it is the same one that Billy and I were watching down by the lake. There, it was going in semicircles and coming back because, as Billy said, it was hunting over water and using the wind to soar. But now it is circling over the trees, using thermals to help it soar. Did I just say that? Did I just say that the sun heats the trees and the ground and the heat rises to create thermals that help the eagle to soar in any direction it wants? And it can go anywhere that its stamina will let it? Did I just say that?

I think I'll just sit back and watch the eagle soar. There must be some kind of prey around, 'cause it just keeps circling overhead. I'll just sit back and watch. It's a beautiful bird. So majestic and graceful. I wonder if it's missing a tail feather?

I've gathered some firewood and built a nice fire. I'm on my first glass of Chardonnay, and it feels good. I've kept my sleeping bag on the right side of the tent, just in case. There's plenty of room. But I'm pissed. Not even a note. He could at least have told me what was going on. Then I would know how to act. Right now, if he should come wandering back, I don't know if I should welcome him back or tell him to just keep on walking. It's incredibly rude to just take off like that. I can handle it. I'm a big girl. What I did, I did because I wanted it. It was my decision. He could have waited and talked to me. Or just left a note. Or, hell with it, maybe left a sign. I'm getting pretty good at that. Just give me a chance. But for now, my glass is empty. I'll have another glass, watch the fire, and see what tomorrow brings.

My sleeping bag is rolled up and in its sheath beside me. The tent is broken down, in its bag, and in the trunk. I'm sitting here at my campsite waiting for my headache to go away. I think it's time to go. Trouble is—I don't know where to go. It was so easy with Billy here. He knew where to go. He took me to places I had never been, that I would never have found by myself. So why the hell did he have to go? Where am I to go now? Should I go east, maybe back home? Should I go west to Flathead Lake and Flathead country? Should I go south to the Bitterroot and the Sawtooth? Should I go north to Canada? My head is numb from the thoughts. But my mind goes back to the ranger talking about trapping a wild animal. What did he say? I remember. "You can capture it or kill it. But sometimes it's better to just let it go."

I lean back onto my rolled-up sleeping bag and look at the sky. It is a bright, clean blue, with some small, puffy clouds. The trees are full and beautiful. And there is an eagle flying high in the sky, west of the campsite. It must be the eagle that Billy and I saw by the lake. The wind is from the north, and it flies south in an arc, flapping its wings to maintain altitude. Then it turns to the north and uses the wind to help it soar, maintaining altitude without flapping its wings, just gliding through the air. The sun has been up for a while, but I don't think there are any thermals. The sun is not high enough and has not had the time to warm the ground and trees. So the eagle continues flying its pattern. But the pattern is slowly moving east, toward me, arced flight to the south and gliding back to the north. Soon the eagle's pattern is right over me.

The eagle arcs to the south again and turns; then it descends a bit, flies straight over me in a straight line, disappears over the trees, and is gone. It is headed north, and if it stays on that path, in ten or twelve hours it could be over Banff. I smile. *If it had the stamina.* I pick up my sleeping bag, throw it in the back seat, hop in the car, and fire the engine. I know where I'm going now. I'm going to the most beautiful place that I have never been. Sometimes it's best just to let it go.

I have to go west to go east. I don't want to go back the way I came. I want to take Going to the Sun Road to travel over the spine of this continent. That road is the main road across and over Glacier National Park. We were on it before, but only for a short time, as Billy wanted to get off the beaten track and go wild. Funny how that phrase came to me.

Going to the Sun Road is spectacular. I'm getting redundant, I know. But what else can I say? I'm glad I'm heading east. The mountain—or mountains—the road is cut out of is mainly to the south slope. To my right is south, the side of the mountain, and to the left is the north, the valleys. So I have a beautiful panoramic view out my driver's side window. Those drivers heading west will have to look out of the right side of the windshield and through the passenger-side window to see the view I'm seeing. If they look out the driver's side window, there is the mountain right next to them. Also, I don't have to worry about going over the side of the mountain as much, as I would have to cross over the other lane before I hit the barrier. This is a narrow and very winding road. And because it is so narrow and winding, no big trailers or long campers are allowed. I'm glad for that. I'd hate to be going ten miles an hour behind a big rig. I'd be less interested, and more pissed off, at watching the tail end of a rig crawling along.

There is not much traffic, so I'm taking it a bit slow

and enjoying the ride. There are a couple of parking lots where you can get out and stretch your legs, but they are at lower elevations, one on each side of Logan's Pass. I'll stop at the one to the east of the pass and get out and enjoy the view. But for now, I'm enjoying the high ride on the top of the world.

I made it over Logan's Pass and am in the parking lot to take a break and enjoy the view. It wasn't as spectacular as at the top of the pass, but it is beautiful, just the same. I get out of the car and stretch. I lean against the car, and the metal is hot from the sun. I don't mind. It feels good on my backside and buttocks. The sun is behind me, and I close my eyes for a moment. I'll need them rested for the ride. When I open my eyes, there is an eagle soaring far in the distance, heading away from me, heading north. A car drives into the parking lot and parks next to me, the radio blasting louder than I would like. I look at the driver—not a dirty look, just a "What the hell?" look. He looks at me, shrugs his shoulders, and smiles. I return my gaze to the north, to the snowcapped mountains and the deep blue sky. I look for the eagle. It is gone. But then again, it might be just over the horizon.

I have passed St. Mary and turned north to Canada. As I look to my left, I can still see the mountains. I feel somewhat sad. Or maybe it's just nostalgia. It was only a couple of days. But I found a freshness, a sort of liberation when Billy was with me. There is beauty, and there is appreciation of beauty. There is watching things being done and doing things. I feel that Billy taught me many things. And I am a better person for it. I am much more confident. I'm not the shy young girl who set out on this voyage. I loved Joe. Perhaps I still do. But Joe always came to me. And with Billy, I was the one that rose from my bedding. I was the one that knee-walked half-naked across the tent. I was the one that raised my shirt. And I was the one that reached down and touched Billy. It is what I wanted, and it is what I took. It would have been nice to have Billy around. But maybe he was just there to show me what I had to learn. Maybe it's better to be on my own now. So I'm heading north and feeling less of what I have lost and more of what I have found.

They are called the Canadian Border Service Agency. They have black shirts, black pants, black ties, black belts, and black shoes, and I believe they wear black socks. On their black hats are the letters CBSA, which are white. The flak jackets are black. They are here to protect Canada from marauders. The traditional uniform was, and still is, blue. But here, black is an option.

I'm at the border, and luckily, there is only one car in front of me. There are two men in black uniforms on either side of that car. It looks like they are finishing up with him as they back away and signal for him to go through. A raised hand and wiggling fingers tell me to move forward. I inch forward until an open palm tells me to stop. The two men stroll to the front windows on either side of the car. I roll down my window.

"Going to Canada, are we, eh?" asks the man by my driver's side window.

"Yes," I manage, noting the man on the left looking through the windows of my car.

"May I see your passport?" he asks. There was a

time when a driver's license would do. But not now. I've studied the rules and know that one is allowed two bottles of wine and twenty-four cans of beer. Actually they are on the metric system, but I was able to convert. I've got a half bottle of wine in my cooler, so I should be okay.

I pick up my passport from the passenger seat and hand it to him. He turns and heads to the guardhouse. I can see him through the window, apparently fingering a computer. In just two minutes, he returns and hands me my passport, along with a folded map. "This is a map of Alberta and British Columbia," he says, extending his hand.

"That's okay," I say. "I've got my GPS."

"Well, that's good," he says. "But sometimes, it may be a little off. You might want to take this, sort of as a backup," he says and extends his map-laden hand.

I take the map. "Yeah," I say. "Thank you."

"You staying long?" he asks.

"I don't know," I say. "I don't think it will be very long."

"Business or pleasure?" he asks.

"Pleasure," I say. "I'm camping."

"And where might you be going, eh?" he asks.

"I'm going up to the lakes around Banff."

"Oh, those are beautiful lakes," he says. "Would you mind opening your boot, eh?"

"Ah ... what?"

"Your trunk. Would you mind opening your trunk, please?"

I fumble with the dash, find the button, and push. I hear a *click* as the man moves toward the back of the car. He lifts up the trunk lid, and I can hear him moving some things around. He pushes the trunk lid down and gently locks it. He turns and comes toward my window, but stops by the back window. "What's in the cooler in the back seat?" he asks.

"Oh, just some food, I guess," I say. "And a bottle of wine."

"Would you mind getting out of the car and opening the cooler?"

I hop out of the car, reach in, and open the cooler. There is a half-filled bottle of last night's wine lying askew in the cooler.

"This left over from last night, I 'magine?" he asks.

I nod. "Yeah," I say. "I figured that if it was in the back seat, you know, out of my reach, it would be okay. It gets a little hot in the trunk, and with the air conditioning on in the back of the car ..."

"It's best to keep it in the trunk," he says. "It'll stay cool enough in the cooler. Would you mind placing it in the trunk? We wouldn't want anything embarrassing up the road."

I pull the cooler out of the back seat, put it in the trunk, and plop back into the driver's seat.

"You going to the Stampede?" he asks.

"Ah, stampede?" I stammer.

"Oh, yeah," he says. "The Calgary Stampede. It's the biggest rodeo on the planet. And you're just in time."

"Well, I hadn't, um ..."

"Well, if you're passing through and you're a rodeo fan, you shouldn't miss it."

"Well, I, ah, I guess ..."

"Just a thought, ma'am," he says. "Anyway, you're good to go." He signals with the back of his hand, and the crossbar lifts. "Have a nice time in Canada, eh?"

I'm lost. I'm standing outside of my car, looking at a

map and cursing the GPS. And unless they are having a rodeo in an apartment complex, I'm in the wrong place.

I hear hoof clops. I look up. Coming toward me in the middle of the street is a Mountie. I don't mean a fake Mountie like you might see in a circus. This is a real live Mountie. This is the RCMP, the Royal Canadian Mounted Police. This is not the new RCMP with their automatic weapons and flak jackets. This is a tall man on a beautiful jet-black horse. It is as if he rode out of a 1950s movie. Make that a 1960s movie to make sure it is in living color. His tunic is bright red, black shoulder epaulets, navy-blue trousers with a yellow stripe down the sides, highly polished black boots. He has a pistol belt around his waist, and its flap-covered holster hides, I'm sure, a six-shooter pistol. A very dark leather strap extends diagonally from his shoulder to his belt. His face is clean-shaven, and his head is topped by a flat-brimmed hat with indentations on the top. This is one good-lookin' Mountie. A handsome man riding a horse in the middle of the city. *Now, why didn't I think of that?*

With a few more *clip-clops*, he approaches and turns toward me. "Can I help you, ma'am?" he asks in a low, masculine voice.

I almost laugh. He is sitting so high on that steed. But I only manage, "Ahh."

"I see you are looking at a map," he says. "And I see that your car has Minnesota license plates. So I wonder if I can be of service."

Now the laugh comes out. Why not? But I manage, "Ah, yes." And that's all I can do.

"Let me guess," he says. "You're looking for the Stampede."

I nod my head. "Yeah," I say. "I'm looking for the Stampede."

"Well, you're not far off," he says. "I think the GPS is off somehow. You're not the first one I've helped."

Composed, I add, "I'm sorry that I laughed. It's just that I didn't expect—"

"Don't worry. This is just my dress uniform. Just for the Stampede. This is a special occasion for us, so we like to show it off, just like it was in the old days." He dismounts and pats the horse on the neck. The horse shivers its mane. "Let me see the map," he says.

I extend the map to his burly fingers. "You are here," he says, pointing. "The Stampede is here," pointing again. He pulls his hand from the map and hands it back to me. He points to his left, to what I think is the west.

"You just go west," he says. "Down this street about a mile or so. Keep your window open. You'll hear it, and your ears will guide you home." He remounts his steed. "Anything else I can help you with?" he asks.

"Oh, I wish," I say under my breath. "No, you've been very kind," I say. "Thank you very much."

He tips his hat to me. "Well, then," he says. "Have a nice time in Canada, eh?"

Chapter 20

I LOOKED UP CAMPSITES NEAR BANFF ON MY PHONE. THERE was a website and a phone number for reserving a site. I called the number and told them I was a tenter. They thought Two Jack Lake campground would be a good place to start. It is close to Banff and probably the first one I would come to anyway. Two Jack Lake is only about two hours away. I am going to stop in at the Stampede to see what's shakin', and I don't know how long I will want to stay, so having a reservation takes a lot off my mind.

I have found the grandstand. I am driving around the parking lot looking for a parking spot. There are some cars, but mainly pickups. There are dumpy old rust-buckets, but mainly nice pickups. Didn't surprise me. This is a rodeo. Most license plates are from Alberta or British Columbia. But there are plenty of cars from the States—New York, Texas, California, all over. The grandstand is nice, bigger than I thought it would be. But, once again, this is the biggest rodeo in the world, or so they say.

I have parked my car and made my way into the arena. The place is packed, but I found a spot with three empty seats. I took the seat in the middle, hoping to keep some elbow room.

Chloe

Nice try.

"Excuse me," says a voice from above.

I turn and see two twenty-somethings in cowboy boots, worn jeans, checked shirts with embroidered pockets and cowboy hats, four beers in four hands.

"I believe you are sitting in the middle of three seats," says the closest cowboy. "We were wondering if you would mind sliding over a seat."

No choice. I slide over one seat, and the two sit down.

"Been to one of these?" asks the closest cowboy as his beer sloshes over the rim of the cup.

"No," I say. "This is my first."

Cowboy One takes a big gulp, lowering the chances of another spill. "Well," he says. "You're gonna love it." Another gulp.

"I'm looking forward to it," I say.

Cowboy Two leans over Cowboy One, spilling his beer on the other's leg. "Yeah," he manages. "You're gonna love it. They got the chuck wagon race comin' up."

I look out onto the field. There is a large track around the perimeter with a grass infield in the middle. Horses are being led around the track to the applause of the audience. Then the horses are led out of the gate, leaving the arena empty. Soon four chuck wagons led by four-horse teams enter the arena. Two barrels are placed at some distance apart.

"See those barrels?" asks Cowboy One, leaning against me.

I nod.

"Those barrels," he continues. "They've got to run around them in a figure eight and then race around the track." He takes another swig and pushes his cup toward me. "Want some?" he manages.

I shake my head and look forward.

"This is gonna be great," he says. "There's lots of

action. Each team has four horses pulling the wagon and a couple of outriders on really fast horses alongside of them pushing them on. When it starts, the outriders have to throw some tent poles and a barrel into the back of the wagon. This sort of represents breaking camp. Then the outriders have to mount up and race around with the wagon. If they get too far behind the wagon, they get time-fined. So it's really a race for not only the wagon, but the outriders as well. That's what makes it so damn fun."

Soon the teams are in position. The loudspeaker sings out, "Take your positions ... ready ..." A flag goes down, and two men from each team throw tent poles and a barrel into the back of the chuck-wagons, and the race is on.

Each team vies for position with outriders urging them on. Horses, riders, and wagons plow into each other, and the crowd roars as if they were at the Roman Coliseum looking for blood. The wagons make the first turn without casualties. At the second barrel, a wagon slams into another wagon, and one of the horses in the second team goes down, now being dragged by the others. The wagon stops as the others pass by. The downed horse tries to get up as the outriders dismount and run to it. One of them takes off his hat and waves it frantically. The horse continues to try to rise, the outriders trying to hold it down, but the horse keeps kicking frantically, its broken leg flailing like a cheerleader's baton. The rest of the contestants continue around the track to the screams of the fans.

"That one is done," says Cowboy Two.

"Yeah," says Cowboy One.

I don't know what to say. "What now?" I ask.

Cowboy One laughs. "Finish the damn race," he says.

"But what about the horse?" I say, pointing to the arena.

"Frickin' shoot him, he's gone," says Cowboy Two, rising and raising his beer cups in some sort of salute.

"No," says Cowboy One, pushing Cowboy Two back into his seat. He turns to me. "Its leg is broken," he says. "It'll have to be euthanized."

"You mean killed," I say.

"Well, that's one way of putting it," says Cowboy One. "With a broken leg, well, it's the best thing for him. This is the fourth one this year."

"The fourth one this year?" I ask, turning to him.

He nods his head and takes another swig of beer.

I turn back to the doomed animal struggling to get up and try to close my ears to the roar of the crowd.

I hate seeing animals suffer. Maybe it's just me. But I don't understand how someone could just keep cheering when an animal is lying there suffering. I just don't understand it. I know it is a different culture and all that. And there is nothing to do for the animal, but jeez. Maybe it's just that I can identify with that animal better than the rest. Maybe my condition makes me different. I know that I may not live a long life. So the animal lies there on the ground, and the crowd keeps cheering. I am here standing, and the world keeps turning.

It only took a couple of hours to drive from Calgary to Banff. I had called ahead and reserved a campsite at Two Jack Lake campsite. When I called ahead, I told them that I was camping alone and would like a more secluded site, if they had one. They did a good job for me. I can still see and hear other campers, but this is a good site. I've walked to the lake and dipped my toes. It is a nice lake. There are trees, of course. And there are mountains galore. The mountains around Banff are a little different from the mountains at Glacier. At Glacier, the mountains are stacked amongst and on top of each other. They are amazingly beautiful, don't get me wrong. But the mountains here seem to just jut out of the ground. There is one mountain that I saw—I think its name is Mount Norquay—right next to Banff. And it is as if the earth just opened up and this huge, I mean really huge, piece of rock just jutted up and out. It is rugged on one side and as smooth as a plain on the other side. It must be great for skiing. And there is a ski resort right at the bottom. I've never seen a piece of the earth just jut out of the earth like that. If you don't believe in plate tectonics, come to Banff. Actually, all the mountains just stick out of the earth here, but Mount Norquay is something else.

I've got the tent up, and it's getting late. I'm getting hungry, and I don't feel like cooking tonight. Billy told me that Banff was a neat town. And the mountains all around it are spectacular. But I think it's time to go into town and have a nice meal at a bar. Now, that sounds like Canada, doesn't it?

I've parked my car on the main street and am looking for a bar. Banff is a nice little town. Really nice. Nestled among the mountains. It definitely has a western feel to it. So tonight I'm going with a burger. A burger and a beer. Or maybe two or three.

Walking the street there are lots of young people. They all look like they are having fun. There are a lot of people my age, but I don't quite feel like carousing with them tonight.   I'll be just me and my burger and my beer.

I find a nice-looking bar called the Elk and Oarsman Pub and Grill. It's upstairs and looks to have a great view. I climb the stairs and enter an old-fashioned bar. There is a bar with stools and tables with chairs.

I don't feel like sitting at a table all by myself. I get enough stares as it is. I find a stool at the bar. I want to fit in as best I can. So I will forsake my glass of wine tonight and will order a beer. I look at the wall behind the bar, and various beer bottles and cans are on display. When I drink beer in the States, I usually drink something light, like Bud or Coors Lite. But I feel frisky tonight, my first night in Canada. And I am going to be camping like a lumberjack tonight. So I peruse the line of bottles behind the bar and very scientifically choose the one with the prettiest label and the prettiest name. It's no contest: Labatt Bleue Dry. I think the *Bleue* is French. How can a wine drinker resist?

Behind the bar is a set of large windows. From the position of the sun, I can tell that I am facing west, maybe northwest. I look out the windows, and there is a great view of Mount Norquay. The front of the mountain has a slope of about thirty degrees, while the back is more like a forty-five-degree pitch. Since it lies to the west, the side facing me is in some shadow, and it looks like a gigantic subterranean shark's dorsal fin sticking about sixteen hundred feet up.

It's not long before a waitress is next to me. She hands me a menu. I take a quick glance, and before she leaves, I ask, "What is the best burger here?"

The waitress smiles. "Ever had a bison burger?" she asks.

"Bison burger?" I ask. "What ..."

"Rather than cow, it's bison," she says. "It's the most popular burger in town."

"Sold," I say. "Medium rare."

The waitress writes on her pad. "And ..."

I look to the back of the bar to make sure I get it straight. "Labatt Bleue Dry," I say.

The waitress's eyes rise from the pad. "You sure?" she asks.

I nod confidently. "That's what the lady wants," I say.

"Got an ID?" she asks.

I pull my driver's license from my purse and hand it to her.

"From the States," she says. "Minnesota. Nice place." She hands me back my driver's license. "First time in Canada?"

"Yeah," I say.

"Sure is beautiful here," she says.

"That's for sure."

"Goin' up to Lake Louise?"

"Tomorrow."

"Don't forget Lake Moraine."

"It's on my list."

"And Emerald Lake Lodge."

"That too."

"Goin' up to Jasper?"

"Don't know yet."

The waitress ponders a moment. "Labatt Bleue Dry," she says.

I nod.

The waitress scribbles on her pad. "Comin' up," she says.

It's not long before a nice-looking young man wearing jeans, a checked shirt, and a cowboy hat takes the stool beside me. He tries to make small talk. I've been jumped and dumped by one cowboy; I don't need another one. Before long, he gets the picture and moves on.

Halfway through my Bison burger, I order a second Bleue. The waitress looks at me and says, "From the States, eh?"

I shrug. "You bet."

"You know that Canadian beer can be stronger than American beers, don't you?"

"Yeah," I say. "I knew that. Hit me."

As I finish my burger, the bartender sidles up to me. "Nice view," he says.

I look out the window. The sun is setting, and the view past Mount Norquay is amazing. I push my empty dish toward him. He picks it up and asks, "Is that it?"

I sort of chuckle under my breath. I look at my second bottle of Labatt's. I can drink half a bottle of wine, so I can certainly handle three beers. My fingers reach out and take the top of the bottle by the lips, turning it so the label faces him.

"Another?" he asks.

Another chuckle beneath my breath and then, "Sure."

Jesus Christ, I'm drunk. But I'm a happy drunk. I start to laugh. I am laughing at nothing. It's not that I have thought of something terribly funny. It's just that

I am laughing at the fact that I am laughing. My tab is paid, and I have left a generous tip. Don't want anyone to think that this American is cheap.

I slide off the bar stool and take measured steps to the door. The bartender is out from behind the bar and beats me to the door. "You all right, ma'am?" he asks.

I chuckle. "I'm fine," I say.

"If you wait for a while, I can take you home," he says.

I wave my hand and make it to the door and down the stairs. The streets are filled with young twenty-somethings. It seems like they are all having fun. I'd probably fit in. But I am not fit to drive. I make it to my car and push a button, and the door clicks open. I open the door and reach down for the trunk release.

Something is knocking at my window. "Go away," I say.

A light is shining in my eyes, and there is knocking on the car window. I open my eyes. There is a man with a flashlight at my car window. He is saying something, but I can't hear him. I close my eyes and turn over. The knocking is louder. I open my eyes again. It is a police officer at the side of my car. I straighten up. I can make out, "Ma'am, please open the door."

What am I to do? I was sleeping in the back seat of my car, which is parked, I think, on the main street in Banff. The officer keeps knocking. I reach over and open the door.

"Ma'am," the officer says. "I will need you to get out of the car."

Well, what the hell. I slide across the seat and get out.

"Have you been drinking, ma'am?" the officer asks.

Well, of course I've been drinking, I think. I open my

mouth and would like to say, "What the hell else would I be doing sleeping in the back seat of my car in the middle of Banff?" but only, "Ah, yes, ah, sir," comes out.

"You know that it is illegal to operate a car while intoxicated?" he asks.

I nod my aching head. "Yes, officer," I say. "But I was not driving my car. I was sleeping in it."

"I see from your license plates that you are from Minnesota," he says.

"Yes, sir," I say.

"Well, if you are in your car and you have access to the keys of the car, then you are considered to be operating the car, even though it is not running."

"Well," I manage though a yawn. "That's just it. I don't have access to the keys."

"Please empty your pockets," he says.

I pull my pockets inside out. Nothing.

"Do you have a purse?"

I reach inside the car and bring out my purse. He takes the purse from me and pokes around inside. "Well, where are the car keys?" he finally asks.

I swallow. "In the trunk," I say.

"In the trunk?" he repeats.

"Yes," I say. "I thought that I might have had a lot to drink, and I did not want to drive. And I did not want to have access to them while I was in the car, so I put them in the trunk and got in the car."

"Well, shit," he says and looks at his feet. "Smart gal. Please open the trunk."

I shrug and click the trunk release.

He walks over to the trunk, opens it, flashes his light, and pulls the car keys from the trunk.

"What were you drinking?" he asks.

"Beer," I reply.

"How many?"

"Three."

"What kind?"

"Labatt's."

"You know that Canadian beers are stronger than American beers?"

"I do now!"

"Well, you were smart to put the keys in the trunk. But we can't have you sleeping in a car on the main street. When did you have your last beer?"

"Ah, about ten o'clock."

"It's two now. Let's see if you're okay. I'm going to stand over there. When I give you the word, you walk toward me with your eyes closed and arms out."

"Okay," I say.

He walks a few paces down the street and turns to me. "Okay, start walking toward me."

I put my arms out to the side, close my eyes, and take a few steps. Everything feels okay. A few more steps and I hear, "Stop."

"You seem to be okay," he says. "Where you stayin'?"

"I've got a campsite at Two Jack."

"That's not too far from here," he says, tossing me the car keys. "Better get a move on, eh."

My head hurts. I open my eyes. The morning sun has warmed the tent, and its brightness makes me close my eyes again. *Big Blue, you gotta help me. You gotta let me know. You've been up here before. I've had three beers before. And I haven't felt this bad since I sneaked some of Dad's hard stuff when I was back in high school. You gotta look after me, Big Blue.* I was supposed to go up to Lake Louise today. I wanted to get an early start, to kind of beat the crowd. But I can't go up there like this, not with my head twice its size.

I take my arm out of my sleeping bag and grab a bottle of Advil. I pop two in my mouth and wash them down with a swig from my water bottle. So I'll just lie here until the Advil takes effect. I'll just lie here for a while. I'll just lie here and close my eyes, just for a while.

Chapter 21

OH MY GOODNESS. THE TENT IS WARM, AND THE SUN IS high. It's late. At least, later than I wanted it to be. But maybe it's for the best. My head doesn't feel like it's under an elephant's foot. I'll just get up, get dressed, and get on my way. A little breakfast, maybe a roll and some orange juice. Throw in a banana, and I'll be on my way. That would save some time. So maybe it's not as late as I think. I think I might have time to just lie here for a minute or two. Just a little bit.

Yeah, I got a late start. I was hoping to beat the crowd up to Lake Louise. I've heard that it is the most beautiful place on the continent. And I really want to see it. But they say that Lake Moraine is really cool too. It is a few miles past Lake Louise. And I don't think most people know about it, at least not as much. I'm sure most people will hit Lake Louise first, as it is the closest. I think I'll go to Lake Moraine first, and maybe when I go to Lake Louise, the crowd will have thinned out.

I park my car in the Lake Moraine parking lot, having bypassed Lake Louise for the moment. I hop out of the car, hit the lock switch, turn left, and hike up the incline to the lake. I can't see the lake yet, but I can see the mountains behind and around the lake. They just jut out of the ground. They remind me of the mountains of the Grand Tetons, just jutting out of the ground. The mountains of Glacier Park were spectacular, to be sure. But those mountains seemed to be piled upon one another more. It's somewhat like having a bunch of Matterhorns stacked up against each other.

On the right is a log building. I think it is a store of some kind. I'll go see the lake first and then check out the store.

As I walk up the parking lot, I see a rushing river to my left. This is obviously the overspill from the lake. At the top of the river is a pile of dead trees, washed over to this area by the tide of the lake. As I walk to the tree pile, the lake comes into view. My, what beauty is this? The lake is surrounded by mountains that jut straight up. The water is emerald green, probably from the glacial silt from the mountains. The view is stark and breathtaking. There is a path to the right. The river, or headwaters of the river, is on the left and makes going that way impossible. There are people taking each other's pictures with the lake and mountains in the background. I ask if I can take a picture for them so all can be in the shot. They accept and ask if I would like to be in my picture. I hand one of them my camera and take a good position. Two or three snaps later, the cameras are returned and we are on our own way. There is a little path to the right, and I go up for a bit of exploring. I find a quiet spot, sit down, and take in this incredible beauty. There are people here, but it is not overcrowded, so it feels like I could just sit down, lie back, and take it all in. It is a beautiful day. The streams of sunlight sprinkle through the trees. Could anything be more beautiful? I guess I'll find out a little bit down the road.

As I pull into the Lake Louise parking lot, signs tell me the main lot is full. No surprise there. I am directed to my left and up a hill to the secondary lot. A car is pulling out from one of the first stalls, so I can save a little on the foot traffic going back to the lake. I park the car and get out. I'm not taking anything with me, as I will just be walking around. I walk down the pavement and round the corner to my left. I am at the back of the main parking lot. There is an incline to the lake, but I cannot see the lake. I can see the mountains behind the lake—and what a sight they are. To the right, up on the hill, is the Chateau Lake Louise. Wow, what a sight. A magnificent structure, right out of a postcard. I walk uphill for a while, and finally, the lake comes into sight. I have never seen anything more beautiful. The lake is emerald green, from the glacial silt. The mountains on either side slant down to the lake, making a V. There is no snow on the mountains on either side, and they are filled with pine trees. But the mountains in back of the lake have snow almost all the way to the bottom, with almost no trees. The tree-covered mountains on either side make a V, as if they are gigantic green curtains, opening up to reveal the beauty of the snow-covered glacier in the back.

There is a platform at the front of the lake, and many people are milling around, taking pictures of the lake. I take my cell phone out of my pocket, click to camera, and take a snap. I will relive this moment whenever I want, but I'm sure the scene is imprinted in my mind. I am sure I will never forget this beauty.

There is no trail to the left around the lake; the pitch is too steep, and much of the ground is rock slide laden. To the right, in front of the chateau, is a trail. The right side is fully treed out and will make for a nice trail up and around the lake. I sit for a while, taking it in. The chateau is beautiful, but I don't have any desire to check it out. It is enough that it is there and I have seen it. There are a couple of benches at the start of the trail, so I sit and take it all in.

After a while, I'm ready for a little hike. Some others have started up to trail, some with backpacks, but most, like me, without. Just a day trip. I start up the trail. It is not a steep climb, more genteel for day-trippers like me.

I figure I am about halfway along the right side of the lake. I am a ways up, but I can see it through the trees. Time for a rest. I haven't seen any other hikers for a while, and I think it will be nice if I can go down to the lake, ya know, just to dip my toes in. I make it down through the trees and am by the lakeshore. I take off my shoes and socks and step into the water. Ooh, it's cold. This is a glacial lake, after all. And the shore is rocky. But after a minute, it doesn't feel too bad. But I've had enough for now. I hop back out of the lake and sit down in the grass next to the trees and the beautiful lake. I lie down and look up to the sky. The sun is bright, and there is mostly clear, blue sky, with just a few puffy, white clouds. I close my eyes. This is what I expected. Actually, it is more than I expected. I want to be part of this. I want to remember this for a lifetime. I look back up to the trail. No one is coming. *I'm going to do it. I'm going for a swim. I'm going to skinny-dip in the most beautiful lake in the world.* I take another look up to the trail. I take off my shirt and bra.

Another look up. Off go my shorts and panties. I make it to the shore and step in. Cold again, but bearable. A couple of steps into the lake and I take a plunge. Cold water all around me. My senses are heightened. I feel a rush of adrenaline. I take a couple of strokes and then turn over onto my back. It is cold on the top of the water, but it's not so bad once you get used to it. In fact, it's kind of refreshing. I look up at the sky and take some back strokes. The water is really clear. I want to be part of this water. I want to dive down deep and swim around in it. I turn over and make a dive. I stroke down, trying to stay perpendicular, inverted, vertical. And even though it is cold, I feel comfortable. I keep stroking down. My ears start to hurt. I take a swallow, and it's okay. Another stroke down, and then another. One more stroke. My hand feels cold water. I mean *really* cold. I stroke with my other hand, and it is as if I hit a wall of icy-cold water, much colder than the water around my body. I turn and look upward. The sun is making its way through the water in fluorescent strobes. I chuckle and rise quickly to the surface. I break the surface, shake my head to get the water off my face, and turn toward shore. After I've dived into the ice water below, the water now doesn't feel too bad. I start to swim toward shore. But after a few strokes, I roll over on my back, so I can see the sky. And I look up at the blue sky and white, puffy clouds. A couple of back strokes and I'm on the shore.

On the shore, I've laid out my clothes and am lying on top of them. I am bare-ass naked, lying in the sun. And I don't care. I want to be part of this. I want to be accepted here for what I am. I hear some giggling up the hill. I look up and can make out a couple on the trail looking down at me. The girl has her hand to her face and is giggling. Her male friend is just standing there, taking in the view. *Go ahead and look. Go ahead and look at a woman in full. I'm here. I am naked. And I am unashamed. And I am alive.*

Then the girl grabs the young man by the arm. The man just stands there. "Come on," I hear from the girl as she tugs at his arm. Finally, he surrenders, and they continue up the trail.

I look up into the sky above the lake. Above the lake, at quite a distance, is a bald eagle. It is flapping its wings as it crosses the water. It is headed in my direction. I lay my head back and close my eyes. I spread my arms out and touch the grass. It is warm. I can feel the heat from the sun on my skin. I open my eyes, and the eagle has crossed the lake and is headed for me. It flaps its wings as it nears the shore and gains altitude. When it is above me, it spreads its wings and glides, making a large circle above me. It seems to be retaining its altitude as it glides, but why doesn't it flap its wings?

I hear a voice faintly in my ear. I can't make it out. It is far away. I can hear it, but I can't make it out. I close my eyes. "What?" I say. "What? I can't make it out."

Clearer, the voice in my head says, "Look ... at ... the ... clouds."

I look out to the clouds above the lake. They are elongated, a little puffy, but with a flat, lateral bottom. I look at the clouds above me. Some have flat, lateral bottoms, but some have a vertical plume, shooting part of the cloud upward.

"Of course," I say to myself. The air above the cold water is stable, causing lateral clouds, but the sun has warmed the trees and the ground where I am, creating an updraft. The eagle can fly around indefinitely without flapping its wings as long as it stays in the thermals. I'm glad that I went to Lake Moraine first. That gave the sun enough time. Enough time that when I got here, the sun had warmed the trees and ground to create an updraft. I smile. "Thank you, Billy," I say softly.

Wow, what was that? My whole body shuddered. Just for a moment. I mean my whole body shook. And then it was gone. *Maybe it just was a reaction to the cold water. Yeah, that has got to be it.* I feel fine now. It only lasted a moment—less than a second, I figure. Just the cold water catching up to me. I'm fine now.

So, I have been seen in my all-together by two strangers. I don't care. I am unashamed. I just want to lie here in the sunshine. I want to be part of this nature. I want to *be* natural. I want to be real. And it finally comes to me. I want to be alive. *I ... love ... life.*

Chapter 22

I'M GLAD I WENT TO LAKE LOUISE SECOND. IF I HAD GONE there first, I would have been chomping at the bit to see Lake Moraine. And even if I had done everything in the same manner, I would have left earlier and not have given the sun enough time to do its work. To stay in the bright sunshine in the most beautiful place I have ever been. To take off my clothes and be part of it, and to lie naked next to it and feel the warm sun on my skin, and to feel unashamed.

There are turning points in everyone's lives. Maybe that was a turning point for me. I feel good now. I feel more alive now than I have ever felt. I love this life. And I want more.

Fully clothed and in my car again, I'm exiting the Lake Louise parking lot. I see a figure with a hat with his arm out, thumb extended. Why not? I pull over, and he ambles to the car, opens the door, and hops in.

"Where to?" I ask.

"Emerald Lake Lodge," he says.

"Where's that?" I ask.

"About forty kilos up Highway 1," he answers.

"Forty, ah ..."

"About twenty miles," he says. "Turn left at Highway 1, at the sign."

I proceed to the entrance of Highway 1 and turn left, away from my campsite at Two Jack, but toward possibly a new adventure at Emerald Lake. I've heard of it, and it sounds nice. I look to my right at the young man in the passenger seat. He's about five-ten, one hundred sixty perhaps. Nice build under that T-shirt. He has a baseball cap on his head, and brown hair flows out of it and reaches below his ears. Looks like two or three days of soft whiskers on his face. He is pleasant-looking, not quite as good-looking as Billy, but you could say that about a lot of guys and still end up with a handful of hunks.

"You staying there?" I ask.

"Yeah," he answers. "I work there."

"Must be a nice place," I say.

"It's gorgeous," he says. "You watch *The Bachelorette?*"

"I take a peek," I say.

"A couple of years back, they had an episode of *The Bachelorette* filmed there," he says.

I think for a minute. Another unreality show. But who am I, Chloe the Clone, to talk about the shadow of reality? "I might have seen it," I say. "Couple of years back?"

"Yeah."

"I remember one episode where they were at a beautiful resort in the mountains by a beautiful lake."

"That's got to be it," he says.

"I just remember it was gorgeous."

"Ah, you're gonna like it," he says.

As the road reaches the top of the pass, he says, "We're passing into BC."

"BC?"

"British Columbia," he says. "We're now in Yoho National Park."

Chloe

We drive a little farther, and he points to a sign up ahead.

"Turn in here," he says.

I turn the car at the sign and follow a paved road. I can see the mountains ahead. One more turn and we are crossing over a pretty bridge running over what looks like a creek. Then to the right is the lodge. And behind the lodge is one of the most beautiful sights I have seen. A beautiful, emerald-green lake surrounded, and I mean totally surrounded, by mountains. It is as if this lake was carved out of a mountain range and nestled in for the gods to bathe in. And the only structures on the lake are the lodge and its outbuildings. If you had to choose between Lake Louise and Emerald Lake, it would be a hard choice. Lake Louise is grandiose. Huge, with a glorious chateau up the right side of the lake and the mountains on either side acting as gigantic, green velvet curtains opening up to a brilliant, snowcapped mountain in the background. The parking lot is large to accommodate the crowds. And people are everywhere.

Emerald Lake is much quieter. It is only there for the guests of the lodge. Or maybe some wanderers like myself. A little off the beaten path, I suppose. But that is what makes it special. It is just as gorgeous, but more secluded. Lake Louise is regal and majestic. Emerald Lake is beautiful and intimate. At Lake Louise, you want to shout to the world. At Emerald Lake, you want to pour yourself a glass of wine and cuddle.

As we pull up to the lodge, I stop the car. "What's your name?" my passenger asks.

"That's a poor effort," I say. "We've been together for about twenty minutes, and I haven't even introduced myself. I'm Chloe."

"I'm Jeff," he says.

Another J-man in my life. What are the odds? "I guess I was so enthralled with the scenery that I forgot my manners," I say.

"It's my fault," he says. "I'm the one that should have introduced myself."

I extend my hand. He takes it and shakes it. "Tell you what," he says. "I imagine, since you have been camping out, how'd you like to take a nice shower? I'll trade you a ride for a shower."

I can almost smell myself. And even with a swim in the lake, I feel the grunge of weeks on the road. "Can you do that?" I ask.

"Yeah," he says. "I work here. Have for quite some time. Sort of in charge of the help. Let's park the car, and I'll get you showered up."

I park the car, and we walk to the lodge.

"I'm in charge of the cleaning crew and the servers," Jeff says. "We get our meals free, unless it's a steak or something. Then it is discounted. I know the chef really well. You can eat off my plate, so to speak," Jeff says. "We are short one cleaning gal. The owner is away for a week. There's a free bed for the night and a ladies' room. If you're tired of sleeping on the ground. It's a bed. And it's safe."

"I swam in the lake earlier but I could use a shower," I say. "As for the bed, let's see about that a little later, after I get used to this place."

"You swam in the lake?" asks Jeff. "You swam in Lake Louise?"

"Yeah, I took a dip."

"Pretty cold, wasn't it, eh?" asks Jeff. "Shrivel your privates, did ya, eh?"

"Boy, you can say that," I say.

"Follow me," he says. "Let's get you to the shower and warm you up, eh?"

Jeff supplies a clean towel, and I take a warm shower in the ladies' quarters. Boy, does it feel great! I am probably using too much water, but it's hard to turn the faucet off and give up this piece of heaven. But I turn off the spigot, towel off, and put my clothes back on. I look around the room. There are a few beds for the female staff. That one bed looks mighty inviting. *Let's have some dinner and see if I land back in here for the night.*

"How was the shower?" asks Jeff.

My hair is still a little wet, but my clothes are warm and dry. "Terrific," I say. "I really appreciate it."

"Wanna go for a walk, eh?" Jeff asks.

"Sure," I say. "Where to?"

"We can walk around the lake a bit," he says.

We have walked along a path near the lake until we are out of sight of the lodge. The lake is beautiful. The clear water is reflecting the bright blue sky. I'm really surprised how much I can see of the bottom near the shore, even though the path is a little way away from the waterline.

"Why don't we go down to the shore?" I ask.

"I was going to suggest that," says Jeff. "I was just waiting for a good spot."

Jeff leads me to the shoreline and picks up a stone to toss it into the lake.

"Don't do that just now," I say. "The water is so clear, and I can see quite a ways out." I pull his arm back. "Let's just sit here and drink this in for a while."

Jeff smiles. "You're right," he says and follows me back a couple of feet.

I sit down, and he sits down next to me. We both pull our feet up and wrap our arms around them, heads on knees. I turn and look at him, with my head still on my knees, and he is looking back at me, head on knees. We both laugh at the sight.

"So," says Jeff. "Tell me about your swim in Lake Louise."

"It was pretty cold when I first got in," I say. "But, once I was in, it didn't feel too bad at all."

"Wait a minute," says Jeff. "I didn't see a swimsuit."

I nod with my chin on my knees. "Didn't have one," I say.

Jeff laughs. "You went skinny-dipping in Lake Louise?" he asks.

I nod. "Actually, I didn't really think of it as skinny-dipping. I guess I just wanted to be part of the beautiful lake, and I didn't have a suit. I didn't want to get my clothes wet, so I just took my clothes off and went in. There was nothing sexual about it. I just wanted to experience it, I guess."

"Were there people around?" asks Jeff.

"Not when I first went in," I say. "But later, yeah."

"Well, what do ya think?" Jeff asks.

"It was wonderful," I say. "The water didn't seem as cold as when I first got in. I swam out for a while, and then I really wanted to dive down deep. I dove down quite a bit, and then I felt this really cold ... I don't know ... it felt like a layer of really cold water all of a sudden."

"You must have hit the thermocline," says Jeff.

"The what?" I ask.

"The thermocline," says Jeff. "It's a layer of water separating the warmer water from the colder water. In northern lakes, like this one and Lake Louise, it can be quite distinct."

"I didn't know that," I say. "I know there is warmer water on top in the summer because of the sunshine and all that, but I thought it would just gradually turn cooler as you go down."

"Well, it does a bit," says Jeff. "But the thermocline is a very distinct layer that separates the different layers, as you experienced."

"That's for sure."

"The water in the bottom of a deep lake like this is always four degrees," says Jeff.

"Wait," I say. "Water freezes at thirty-two degrees."

"Sorry," says Jeff. "We're in Canada. We use Celsius. I'll change to Fahrenheit." Jeff thinks for a moment. "So, four degrees Celsius would convert to ... let's see ... around thirty-nine degrees Fahrenheit. Fresh water is densest at thirty-nine degrees. And since it is densest, it will be the heaviest and sink to the bottom. The water on top of the lake is the warmest, therefore is the lightest and will stay at the top. There are various layers separating them, but the most distinct layer is the thermocline."

"What about in the winter, when the water on top is colder? Wouldn't the water at the top be colder and therefore, more dense?"

"Actually, no," says Jeff. "Warm water will be less dense, and the molecules are farther apart. As the water cools, the water gets more dense until it reaches thirty-nine degrees. And as it gets colder than thirty-nine degrees, it becomes less dense. That is why ice floats, because water at thirty-two degrees is less dense than water at thirty-nine degrees. And in the spring, as the ice melts and the water that was thirty-two degrees warms to thirty-nine degrees, it will be denser and sink to the bottom of the lake. And the top of the lake will warm up again, and you can have a swim."

"That's fascinating," I say. "I guess I learned something today."

"Want to go for a swim?" asks Jeff.

I look over to him. He has turned to me and has that look on his face.

"No," I say. "One swim per day is enough."

Jeff has introduced me to the staff, and I am helping the servers set the tables and clean off the tables when the patrons are done with their dinner. I don't mind helping, especially when there is a nice, hot, restaurant-quality meal promised me for my work. It's interesting to see how professional the servers are. There is just the right amount of banter with the patrons to keep the pace. I admire their proficiency. I hear the clatter of the plates and the clinking of the silverware as they prepare the next table to be seated. And when the patrons are done with their dining and the check has been paid, I am there to clear the table and bring the dirty dishes to the kitchen. And the process begins again. I like this place. I like the lodge and I like the people and I love the lake. I think this would be a good place to spend the night. I can't wait to see how the sun looks as it comes up over the mountain.

The patrons are gone. I'm sitting at a dinner table with Jeff. The other gals are at a different table and paying no attention to us. Apparently, they are giving free rein to Jeff. Or maybe they are just not that interested. Anyway, Jeff and I are having a nice dinner together. The dinner was free, and Jeff has sprung for a nice bottle of Chardonnay. I've got scallops, mashed potatoes, and a nice vegetable medley, half on my plate and half in my belly. The mountain air can really give you an appetite. Though I am still hungry, I slow the pace a bit, just to maintain appearances. Jeff asks me about the food. I nod my head and lift my fork in acknowledgement. "It's terrific," I say and take another sip of wine.

When we are done with the meal, Jeff asks if I would like some pie. "Not tonight," I say. "The meal was fantastic."

Jeff lifts the bottle of wine. "There's still enough for another glass," he says and offers the bottle to me, but then pulls it back. He looks around to the other help, chatting away at a nearby table.

"We could take this out to the lake," he says.

Yeah right, like I don't know what's coming. But what the hell, I'm a big girl. And wine by the lake sounds nice. I smile and nod. "Sounds nice," I say.

Jeff puts the cork back in the bottle, rises with the bottle by his side, away from the other girls, and nods toward the door. I look at the girls, and they are too busy in conversation to notice us. I turn my back to them and deftly pick up our two wineglasses. A few steps and we are out the door.

I follow Jeff down the path we followed earlier. I hear the clink of the glass and giggle to myself. We are out of sight of the lodge and find a nice place by the lake to sit. Jeff bites down on the cork and wrests it from the bottle. I hold out both glasses as he empties the bottle. We turn to the lake. It is beautiful. The moon is full and bright tonight, and the reflection glistens off the lake. I'm somewhat surprised that I can still see the emerald color of the water in the semidarkness. There is a warm, gentle breeze coming off the lake. I take a sip, sitting with my legs up to my chest. Jeff leans back on one elbow, holds out his glass, and offers me a toast. "To a beautiful evening," he says.

"To a beautiful evening," I rejoin and clink his glass with mine.

"How do you like your stay here so far?" Jeff asks.

I take a sip. "I love it," I say. "I never realized how beautiful the mountains could be. I really love it here."

"How long do you plan on stayin', eh?" he asks.

"I don't know," I say. "I have to go pick up my tent tomorrow down at Two Jack. I'm only paid through tonight."

"Plannin' on comin' back?" he asks.

I rest my chin on my knee. "I don't know," I say.

I see a small sapling down by the lakeshore. It looks like all other saplings, except this one looks like it is growing out of a boulder by the shore. I point to it.

"Look at that tree," I say. "It looks like it is growing right out of a rock.

"Yeah," says Jeff. "It probably germinated in a crevice and has grown from there."

"But there is no earth there," I say. "No ground."

"There's enough," says Jeff. "I've seen trees that were growing between two large boulders. And yet the tree is strong enough to move the boulders. It's amazing, the power of a growing tree."

"It's such a pretty little tree," I say. "Do you think it will last?"

Jeff gets up and walks to the tree, takes a look, comes back.

"Nah," Jeff says as he sits down next to me. "Stone's too big. Not enough dirt. Try as it might, it won't last."

We have finished our glasses, and they are on the ground. Jeff straightens up and slides over next to me. I know what's coming, and I lower my knees. Jeff puts his arm around me, and I turn to him. He kisses me fully on the lips, and I accept. He adjusts his position next to me, and we kiss. I've not been with a man since ... since Billy. Jeff is not Billy, but he is a man. I like the way his half-beard rubs against my face. The stubbles are soft but still give a manly feel as they rustle against my cheek. I listen for footsteps, and there are none. We kiss deeply again.

I gather myself and take a breath. "Jeff," I say. "I think that's enough."

Jeff pulls back. "I thought you were ..."

"I was, Jeff," I say. "I really like you. Here in the moonlight, and the lake and ... everything. But that's enough."

Jeff pulls back like a chastised child.

"It's okay, Jeff," I say. "Maybe another time."

His right hand recedes to his lap, but his left hand is still around my back. I softly put my head against his shoulder. His left cheek lies against the top of my head, and together we look at the mountains and the moon as we snuggle by a lake the color of a gemstone.

Chapter 23

I AWAKEN TO THE SOFT MEMORIES OF THE NIGHT BEFORE. I hear the shower in the bathroom. My head does not feel any effect from the wine. In fact, I feel really good. And I'm wondering what I should do about Big Blue. I've got to break camp by noon today. But this is such a nice place. Jeff has been great. Could have been better than great if allowed. But I'll settle for great for now. I hear the shower turn off. *Boy, it would be nice to take another shower here.* I'm really thankful for the gals in here. They welcomed me but left me alone. I like helping them in the dining room.

The bathroom door opens, and Greta steps out, a towel covering her body. She is a nice-looking blonde, maybe twenty-five or so, with a nice figure. She throws me a towel and tells me the shower is open if I want it. She knows I'm just a vagabond and have no toiletries with me. She tells me there is soap in the shower and she has left her shampoo for me. I thank her, hop out of bed, and head for the shower.

I towel off as best I can and head back to my bed. My body is clean, but my hair is a mess. I don't even have a comb. Greta looks at me and laughs. "You should see yourself," she says with a giggle.

I wander over to the mirror by Greta. I look at my wild-haired reflection, bring up my right hand to make a claw, and growl. Greta chuckles. I think she likes me.

"Here," says Greta, holding up her hair drier. "Try this."

"Thanks," I say, adjusting my towel closely to my body. I take the dryer and use my fingers as a comb.

"Want to use my comb?" asks Greta.

I don't think that would be very good. I'm thinking of Greta. I shake my head and thank her. But Greta is looking at me. She is giving me that look. "What?" I ask.

Greta just smiles and shakes her head. "Nothing," she says, turns, and walks out the door.

In a few minutes, my hair is dry, and it doesn't look too bad. A little wildness never hurts. We're in the mountains, aren't we? I saunter over to my bed. I take off the towel and slip my panties on. Then I reach into my bag and take out my bra. I've been braless for a while, and it was a fun and light and breezy, sort of a feeling of freedom. But now it's time to saddle up. I'll be helping in the dining room, and I think it would be more appropriate. Quickly, my shorts, shoes, and T-shirt are on, and I'm out the door heading for the dining room.

Jeff sees me as I enter the dining room and gives me a wink. I smile and return the wink. I quickly start to dress the tables with dishes and silverware and napkins. Jeff casually comes by and asks how I slept. I assure him it was good. He smiles and goes back to directing traffic.

I ducked out as soon as I thought it appropriate. I

have to get back to Big Blue by noon, and I don't want to be late. I don't know what I'll do then; but for now, I have just enough time to go down to the lake, to our spot by the lake. And I want to go down there by myself. I don't know if I will tell Jeff that I will be gone, or ask if I can come back. But that's a decision that I have to make by myself. Alone.

I am sitting in our spot by the lake, my legs folded up and my head on my knees. Did I say "our spot?" Why do I think it is "our spot?" Has Jeff brought others here? Have they sat beside him and felt the soft bristles of his unshaven cheek against theirs? Has he placed his lips on theirs, and have they felt his hand wander under their shirts? What am I thinking about? Why should I care? Jeff is here, and there are other women here. Certainly Greta is attractive enough. And I'm sure she's felt his soft whiskers against her cheek. But she doesn't seem to mind that I'm there. She even gave me a towel and her hair dryer. So what am I thinking about? Do I have feelings for Jeff? I don't know. If I do, they're not the same as my feelings for Billy. In the meantime, I think I'll just sit back and admire the sun and the mountains and the lake—and the bald eagle that is flying across the lake. The eagle that started going across the lake from east to west, but banks to its right in a slow, sweeping motion and turns south—south toward Big Blue.

I can't just leave without saying goodbye. I'm back at the lodge. In the dining room, every table is filled. I probably should have stayed to help, but I really needed to work some things out. And the deal was a ride for a shower and some bussing for a dinner. I see Jeff talking to Greta in the kitchen. I walk over to the swinging saloon-type doors. Jeff sees me and turns. "Hi, Chloe," he says. "I was wondering if you had left. Then I saw your car was still here."

"Yeah, I went for a walk by the lake," I say.

Jeff nods his head. I think he knows what's coming. "Goin' to pick up your tent, eh?" he says.

I nod. "Yeah, it's time for me to go," I say. "It's probably a two-hour drive, and if I leave now, I can just make it."

"Yeah," says Jeff.

"I'd like to thank you for your hospitality," I say. "I had a wonderful time here."

"Yeah, it's a special place," says Jeff.

"Yes, it is," I say.

Greta squeezes by me through the door. "'Scuse me," she says, and lets the door swing. Jeff stops it with one hand.

"You could come back," Jeff says. "We could use another hand. I could talk to the owner."

I shrug my shoulders. "We'll see," I say.

Jeff beckons to me with his hand and takes a step back. My left hand swings the door back, and I am next to Jeff, alone in the kitchen.

Jeff looks out to the dining room and then back to me. "I really wish you could stay," he says.

I shake my head slowly. "I don't know," I say.

Jeff nods. "Then that's it?" he says.

I shrug my shoulders. "Maybe," I say. "Let me get out on the road, and we'll see."

"Okay," says Jeff. He pulls me to him and puts his arms around me. "Have a good trip," he says.

I put my arms around him. "Yeah," I say.

"Table five needs some help." Greta's voice is heard from the other side of the saloon doors.

"Yeah," says Jeff and turns to Greta. "I'll be right there."

"Okay," he says. "You go. Maybe we'll see you again."

"Yeah," I say and just stand there.

Jeff gives me one last hug and turns toward table five.

I lied when I told Jeff that I had to leave now to make it back to my campground. I've got a little time before I go. I just wanted a little extra time. To kind of look around. I'm wandering around the grounds to take in one last look at this gorgeous part of Eden.

"Hey," says Jeff from behind.

I turn around. "Hey, back," I say.

"One last look around?" asks Jeff.

"Yeah," I say. "I want this imprinted in my brain."

"Can I show you around a little before you go?"

"Sure."

We stroll together down a walkway in front of a garage.

"This is our garage," says Jeff, nodding.

I look into the garage. There is a red snowblower sitting in the middle of a stall. "Little early for a snowblower," I say.

"Ah, it's broken," says Jeff. "Got a flat tire. Haven't got around to fixin' it yet."

"Well, that should not be a problem," I say.

"Well, yeah, it is," says Jeff. "This is a pneumatic tire. No inner tube. If there was a tube, I could just fish it out and put a new one in and then pump it up. But this tire doesn't have a tube. The tire bead sits on the wheel rim and creates a seal. Then air is pumped in, and we have a useable tire. But the bead came off the rim, and I can't get it back on. Have to take it in and have someone with some know-how take care of it."

"How did the bead come off the rim?" I ask.

"Had a bad snowstorm last spring," says Jeff. "Really wet snow. I was blowin' out the sidewalk and tried to twist and turn the thing around, but the tires were stuck. And I twisted so hard the tire bead came off the rim of the wheel. Now the tire is just lyin' there loose in the wheel. I've got the axle up on a block to keep the wheel off the ground."

"Well, somehow it got on there in the first place," I say. "Has to be a way to get it back on."

"Oh, I'm sure there is, but it's beyond my pay grade," says Jeff. "I'll just take it into town and get it fixed."

Jeff turns and starts down the path. I stand looking at the snowblower. Jeff turns back and looks at me. "What?" he says.

I am looking at the snowblower with its tire disconnected from the wheel. I am thinking about what Billy said: "A man looks at something and sees what it is. A wise man sees what it can become." As I look at the snowblower, I envision the tire. In my mind's eye, I see the tire bead expand and go back onto the wheel rim. I go over and touch the tire, feel the hard rubber and tread. I push down. Nothing happens. I think of a balloon, a round balloon. I think about putting my hands around the circumference of the balloon and squeezing. I see the ends of the balloon being pushed out. What was it Billy said? I see the tire off the rim of the wheel. And I envision the circumference of the tire being pushed down and the sides with their beads expanding up and outward.

I turn to Jeff. "Do you have any rope here?" I ask.

"What?" asks Jeff.

"Rope, do you have any rope?"

"I s'pose. What kind of rope?"

"Any kind. Clothesline will do." I hold out my hands at arm's length. "About this much."

Jeff goes over to a bin, opens it, and brings back a coil of rope. I take it and unravel a little more than twice an arm's length. "Do you have a knife?" I ask.

Jeff pulls a folding knife from his pocket and hands it to me. I open the knife and cut the rope. I hand the knife back to Jeff. I drape the rope around the tire's circumference, following the middle of the tread around the wheel. When the ends of the rope meet, I pull them tight and make a knot.

"Do you have a piece of wood, maybe a stake, or even a tire iron?" I ask.

Jeff looks at me somewhat weirdly but then saunters over to the bin and pulls out a wooden stake. He holds it up. "Will this do?" he asks as he walks toward me.

"Perfect," I say, accepting the stake.

I put the stake perpendicular to the rope around the circumference of the tire. I lift the rope slightly and slip the stake under the rope, perpendicular to the tire, with the point of the stake away from me. I twist the stake. There is a lot of resistance, but I get the stake to rotate so the point is pointing at me. Another twist and the stake rotates so the point is away from me. The rope is taut against the tread of the tire. I make another twist, this time a full 360-degree twist. I see the middle of the tread of the tire sink in a bit. I continue to twist, one after another, and with each twist, the middle of the tire tread sinks and pushes the bead of the tire out and up. Quite a few more twists and the bead is up next to the tire rim. Two more twists and the bead is on the tire rim and expands to the edge of the rim, firmly creating a seal. While still holding the stake, I look all around the tire to make sure the seal goes all around. I slowly unravel the coiled rope, and the tire tread pops back to normal.

"Well," I say. "It looks like we have the tire back on the rim again, and it looks like we have a nice seal. Do you have a pump?"

Jeff just stands there, looking at the tire.

"Do you have an air pump?" I ask again.

"Ah, yeah," says Jeff. "Yeah, I'll get one."

Jeff turns away, goes to the back of the shed, and returns with an air pump. He looks at the side of the tire to get the correct PSI, connects the air hose to the nozzle, and starts to pump. He says over his shoulder, "That's amazing. Who taught you that?"

I think of Billy, and seeing not only what something is, but what something can become. I smile and say, "A very wise man."

Chapter 24

So, I've picked up another hitchhiker who took me to a place of beauty that I've never been before. This is getting to be a habit. I turn my car onto Highway 1 and head south. I'll go back to the campsite, pick up Big Blue, and head out. That always had a nice romantic ring to it. But head out to where? I've got some time to think about it. The campsite is around two hours away, I think. I should have some extra time to lie in my tent and think about things. Maybe something will come to me. Maybe Big Blue will help.

It didn't take as long as I thought to reach my campsite. Big Blue was there waiting for me. I slipped out of my car, unzipped the netting, and lay down on my sleeping bag. The sun has warmed the tent, and the sleeping bag is warm to my skin.

The tent has the smell of warm nylon.

I'm thinking back to my father's funeral, sitting there with my brother and sisters. I know now they are not my siblings. But I don't know how to consider them as anything else. And my father. How can I think of him as anything but my father? That is how I grew up. That is how I knew my whole family. Am I different from what I was before I knew? No. I am not different. I have a different knowledge of myself and everyone I know and care about. But to think my father loved my mother so much that he could not bear to live without her. But what does that make me? Am I my mother? Did my father love me because I am the woman he loved? I can't think of it that way. And I know my father did not think of me that way. But how did he think of me, since he knew what I was all along? And how can I have a feeling of myself—I mean, a feeling of who I am? Can I be a separate person with this shadow cast over me? Can I just be myself? And can they love me for being just that? Myself? Let me close my eyes and think, just for a moment. Wait. All the people I know, know me as Chloe. Nothing else. They know me as the person I am. Billy did not make love to a freak of nature. Jeff did not take a freak of science down to the lake. They did not take some remnant of a banned medical experiment. They took *me*. They took Chloe. They took a vibrant, attractive human being to be with them. I am me. I am *Chloe!*

I lie back with my eyes closed, thinking about the night before. And the day before that. And Jeff holding me. And Billy showing me. And all the wonderful things I feel about myself. My body shakes. Just for a moment, but it really shakes. It was something like the shivers that I had by Lake Louise. And once before that. It only lasted for a millisecond or so. But it shook my whole body. I feel okay now, but this has happened twice before. Maybe it's time to head out. Maybe it's time to start back. I open my eyes and take a deep breath. "What do you think, Big Blue?" I ask. I wait for an answer. No answer. Just the rustle of the wind blowing through the trees and rustling the sides of the tent. It's time to head out. Time to go south.

Well, I'm out of the mountains and have Calgary in my sights. Calgary is an interesting city, perhaps the most interesting city I have been to. I really love Banff, but that is just a town. Calgary is a city. It lies next to the foothills of the Rockies. To the west are the mountains, and to the east are the high plains. Canadian Highway 1, or the Trans-Canada Highway, runs from east to west right through the city. It sort of parallels the Bow River, which comes down from the western mountains and runs to the east, through the city. It is kind of funny: as you follow it upstream past a dam, it turns a sharp right and widens. This is called the El-Bow. Get it?

What I find interesting, coming out of the mountains, is the number of trees in the mountains compared to their scarcity on the High Plains. When you consider that the mountains are mostly rock and the High Plains are mostly grasslands, it makes you wonder. In the mountains, I have seen trees that look like they grow right out of the stone detritus, their roots obviously wedged deep into crevices. And yet there is much more fertile ground on the plains. It just shows how forceful and magnificent these trees are, struggling and grasping at anything for life. And doing it successfully. If you have no appreciation for the forces that nurture and sustain life on this planet, go out to the mountains.

Another thing I like about Calgary is the Stampede. It is not on the outskirts of the city. It is right downtown, only a mile or so south of Highway 1. It's an easy side trip for me. When I was there a few days ago, I don't think I gave it my best. I was upset about the chuck wagon races and the horses being maimed. I'd like to see more of it now that that is over. I think I'll stop by and give it another try.

I'm at the stadium again. I'm going to get into this a little better. I've stopped at the concession stand and bought a cowboy hat. Back home, I may call it a cowgirl hat, but here in Calgary, at the Stampede, it's a cowboy hat. I've curled the brim a little more. That's the way they wear them here. And I've bought a cup of beer. Why not?

I make my way up the stairs and find a seat in the grandstand. I'm sitting next to a couple of cowboys, and they tip their hats to me. I tip mine back. I'm a cowgirl now.

"My name's Jack," says the cowboy next to me.

"I'm Chloe," I say.

"From the States?" he asks.

"How could you tell?" I say.

Jack just smiles and offers me a toast. "Welcome," he says and extends his plastic beer cup.

I press my cup to his. "Thanks," I say.

"Been here before, eh?" he says.

"Few days ago," I say. "Watched the chuck wagon race."

Jack shakes his head. "Damn shame," he says.

"Yeah," I say. "Damn shame."

"I think you'll like this better," he says.

"I hope so," I say. "That's why I came back."

"You got here just in time," he says. "This is the bareback horse riding event. No horses goin' to be hurt here."

"I'm glad of that," I say. "So the riders just ride bareback?"

Jack nods. "Yeah," he says.

"Cool," I say.

"Normally, when men are bareback riding, it is really exciting," says Jack. "There are no saddles, and the rider just sits on the back of the horse. There is a small handle that the rider holds onto, and he tries to hang on as the horse tries to buck him off. Sometimes the horse wins; sometimes it don't."

"And nothing happens to the horse?" I ask.

"Nah," says Jack. "The horse just gets another bale of hay."

"I like it," I say.

"But today is different," says Jack. "Today we have a woman riding bareback."

"Wow," I say.

"But this is a little different," says Jack. "Quite a bit different. I've seen this gal before. She's really good. Name's Stacy Westfall. And rather than bucking, she will just ride around with no saddle and no handle or strap. Nothing to hang onto. Just the horse and her."

"Well, that's simple," I say.

"Ever tried to ride a horse without a saddle or reins?"

"Nope," I say.

"Well, sit back and enjoy," says Jack.

The loudspeaker crackles and then introduces the next rider, Stacy Westfall, riding a horse named Baby Doll. A gate opens, and a black horse trots out with a young girl on its back. The announcer introduces her and relates that the rider would like to dedicate this ride—he pauses as his voice breaks and then continues—to her father, who recently passed away.

The crowd makes an appreciative applause. The horse takes a few steps forward. Stacy is rubbing Baby Doll's mane. The sound of Tim McGraw's "Live Like You Were Dyin'" rings out from the loudspeaker. The jet-black horse moves to its right, laterally a few paces. Then it comes left a few paces. You can see Stacy's lips move, and the horse walks forward; then it twirls quickly in place to the right, followed by swift twirls in place to the left. The crowd roars. The horse trots forward for a while and then takes off at a racing pace, Stacy holding on with just her legs pressed against the sides of the horse. The crowd roars again. The horse and rider take off again at full speed. The horse comes to a full stop with hooves digging in the sand like a speeding car screeching to an emergency stop on a freeway. And then the horse backs up, moving swiftly and directly backward, step by step, like a tightrope walker sensing danger. The audience is on its feet. Everyone. And the roars from the crowd are growing louder. Horse and rider race around the infield a couple of times, going faster with each lap. The crowd is at a fever pitch, and the loudspeaker has raised the volume, blaring out "Live Like You Were Dyin'." Finally, horse and rider come to a stop in the middle of the arena. With no saddle, bridle, or reins, Stacy shifts her weight, bringing her left knee up to the horse's spine. Then her right leg is on its back, and to the roar of the crowd, Stacy Westfall rises up and is standing upright on the back of Baby Doll, arms lifted to shoulder height. The crowd is going wild. Stacy is on the back of the horse, facing to the side, to my side. It's almost as if she is looking at me. Standing upright on the back of this magnificent black animal, she slowly raises her arms to the sky. The noise from the crowd is even drowning out the blaring of the loudspeaker. I am jumping up and down. The beer in my left hand spills, and I don't care. I take off my cowboy hat with my right hand and jab it high into the air as I yell at the top of my voice, *You go, girl!*

Chapter 25

WHAT A SHOW! I CAN'T GET OVER THAT GIRL, STACY, AND how she had command of her horse. No saddle, no reins, just horse and rider as if they were one. And the crowd reaction, and my reaction, as she sped around the arena and the song blaring from the speakers, it seemed to increase as the crowd and I started yelling at the top of our voices. And the song, "Live Like You Were Dyin'." It was perfect.

And the song keeps ringing in my memory. "Live like you were dyin'." Who knows? I don't know how much time I have. And what's with those shimmies? I've had three of them, and I don't know what they are. Maybe it's a … I don't know. I know I'm not, well, normal. Maybe something's going on here. Maybe I don't have a normal life span, a normal time. Maybe I'm taking things for granted. I'm not going to throw caution to the wind and live recklessly. I'm not going to, as Motley Crue's "Kick Start My Heart" put it, "skydive naked from an aeroplane." But that song I heard at the arena meant something to me. Maybe I should look at things a little differently.

Well, I've found my way to Highway 2. I'm headin' south, back to the States. It's been bright and sunny most of the trip, but it's clouding up now. Storm's a-comin'. I'll get as far as I can go.

Hard rain is pelting my windshield. It's really dark, and I've slowed to around thirty miles per hour. I probably should pull over and sit this one out, but I hate sitting on the side of the road. At least I'm moving. The windshield wipers are slapping against the raindrops. I can see enough to keep going.

Through the rain, I see some yellow flickering by the roadside. As I get closer, there are two figures in yellow rain slickers by the side of the road. Caution tells me to just keep going. I don't know who these people are. And what they can do. There are two of them and only one of me. But my humanity tells me to pull over in this downpour.

I come to a gentle stop by the shoulder of the road. The two figures eagerly reach for the rear door handle and open it. They are fumbling with their backpacks, trying to put them in before themselves.

"Wanna put them in the trunk?" I ask.

"Yeah," says the first one.

I push the trunk release on the dash and hear the *click* of the trunk opening. They move around to the back, sloshing in the rain, deposit their backpacks in the trunk, and jostle into the back seat.

"Thank you," one of them says.

"Pretty wet out there," I say.

"Sure is," says the other.

They are young women, about my age, I would say. Nice-looking. And wet. They push their hoods off, and I can see their wet hair and raindrops still on their faces.

"Thank you so much," says the girl on left. "You are a godsend."

"I'm Chloe," I say.

"I'm Mary," says the one on the right.

"I'm Jane," says the one on the left.

"Well, nice to meet you," I say. "Where you headed?"

Jane pulls the wet hood off her head and shakes her hair. "We're on our way to Waterton Lakes," she says.

"Waterton Lakes?" I ask.

"Yeah," says Mary. "It's the Canadian side of Glacier Park."

"I spent some time in Glacier," I say. "Where you from?" I say.

"We're from Portland," says Jane, leaning forward. "We're just on a backpacking trip. We got caught in the rain, and, ah, here we are."

"You don't have a car?" I ask.

They look at each other for a moment. "No," says Mary. "We just wanted to be free spirits for a while."

"And see where that takes us," adds Jane.

"Well," I say. "It'll take you to Waterton." I turn to the front, put the car in gear, and put my foot to the pedal.

"I think you take a right here," says Mary. I can hear her shuffling a folding map.

I turn right onto Highway 5.

"It's not too far now," says Mary, spreading the map out on her lap. "There's a campground just past the town of Waterton."

Jane is looking at a map of campgrounds and agrees with Mary. "There's a lot of campgrounds, but a lot of them are for camper trailers and such. Quite crowded, I would imagine. But there is a campground on something called Bertha Lake, just west of Waterton Lake. It looks like it could be a little quieter."

We arrive at the park entrance. We have had a really nice chat along the way. Both of them are quite gregarious and grateful for the ride. And I like their company.

The weather has cleared, and the sun is out. It is hot again. I park the car, and the three of us get out. Mary and Jane are dry now and have shed their rain slickers. Each has on shorts, a T-shirt, and hiking boots. Both are quite attractive, possibly the same age as me. I take the lead and walk to the ranger station. Inside, we are greeted by a nice female ranger in green shorts and shirt.

"We were wondering," says Jane to the park ranger, "where a good place to camp is."

"What are you looking for, big campsites or smaller, quieter campsites?" asks the ranger.

"We like small, intimate campsites, if you have one," says Mary. "We saw Lake Bertha on the map, and that looked nice."

The ranger nods her head. "If you're looking for a nice, quiet campsite, that would be a good one," she says. "It's a hike from the town of Waterton. You can park your car and hike to the campsite. There are a couple of others, like Carthew, but that's a little farther down the road. Bertha is closer to town if you need supplies."

"Actually, we were looking for a campsite that we could drive to. I have a cooler, so ..." I say.

"Well, the biggest campsite you can drive to is in the town of Waterton. You could get supplies and stuff. Give me a minute," she says and turns to her computer.

"Actually, that campsite is full. It's the only one that you can get a reservation for. The others are first come, first serve. But there is one before you get to the town. Crandall campground is about a few kilometers off Highway 6. It gets pretty windy up there, and a lot of people don't like the wind. But it's the closest one for you that you could drive to. There may be a site for you there."

I turn to Mary and Jane. "Sound okay?" I ask.

"Sounds good to us," says Mary. "Should we pay here?"

The ranger gives the rate, Mary hands the ranger a credit card, and the deal is done.

We drive down Highway 6 for a while and come to a sign for Red Rock Parkway pointing to the right. We take it and drive a couple of miles. The campsite is primitive, and I can't see any trailers parked at the campsite and just a couple of other cars parked by small tents. Apparently, this is really out of the way. I'm kinda surprised that there are not more campers here. The ranger said all the campsites fill up quickly. I think all the other campsites in the park have lake access. This one does not. It is high up in the mountains, and I'm sure it gets windy. But for us, this looks perfect.

I drive to a campsite, park the car, and push the button on the dash. The trunk lid opens with a *click*. Mary and Jane are out of the car and getting their gear out of the trunk. I lean my head back on the headrest, close my eyes, take in a big breath, hold it for a moment, and let it out slowly. It's been a long ride.

I open the door and hop out. "You got your gear?" I ask.

"Yup," they say in unison again.

I notice they each have a backpack. And that's it.

"Where's your tent?" I ask.

"Skunk got it this morning," says Mary.

"Skunk?" I ask.

"Yeah," says Jane. "After breakfast this morning, we took a hike. When we got back, a skunk was in the tent. I guess we scared it, and it sprayed the entire tent. No way you can get that smell out of nylon. Good thing we had all of our gear out, especially our sleeping bags."

"Well, that's a pisser," I say.

I look at these two young women. About my age, nice-looking. Friendly. Alone in the Rocky Mountains without a tent.

I can't conceal a laugh. I reach in my trunk and bring out Big Blue. I can see their eyes wander over to the blue nylon bag next to me. "By the way," I say. "This just happens to be a three-man, or in this case, a three-woman tent. Care to join me?"

Big Blue is a big tent. Too big for backpacking into the back country, but fits perfectly into the trunk of a car and pitches nicely on the open campsite we have found. Its sides are about two feet high, and the roof slants gently to the top, leaving plenty of room to stand up and move around. There are two poles, one in the front and one in the back, so there is plenty of room for three sleeping bags. Clothesline ropes act as guy lines, to pull the sides and keep the tent erect. If the tent were a ship and the front opening were the prow, I would have the port side, and Mary and Jane can divvy up the starboard and middle slots. I like to sleep on my left side so when I roll over, I'm facing the side of the tent, rather than my newfound compatriots. Even with the three sleeping bags, there is plenty of room in the back of the tent for backpacks and sundries.

After pitching the tent and getting organized, Mary and Jane take a hike down a trail. I'm too tired from the drive to go along and am content to sit in our campsite and read a book. I really like this place. It is quiet and away from the hustle and bustle. A few campers, just a few places for tenters like us. There are a couple of other tents down a ways, but I haven't seen anyone else. Lots of beautiful trees and bright blue skies and a warm, gentle breeze. I think I'll just sit back and read a bit.

Mary and Jane have come back from their hike, gathered firewood, and built a nice fire in the fire-pit. They have offered me a packet of freeze-dried food, something with rice and chicken, I suspect. We boil three packets in a small pan of water over one of their camp stoves.

I pull a bottle of Chardonnay from my cooler and ask if they have any glasses. Jane goes to the tent and comes back with three plastic cups. She sits down on a log next to Mary, across from me. I unscrew the cap and fill each cup. They thank me and take the food bags out of the pan, open mine, and put it on a plastic plate. I must admit, it tastes better than it looks. I raise my cup for a toast. Three plastic cups clink across the campfire flames. I take a sip. Mary is apparently right-handed, as she holds the cup in her right hand. Jane holds her glass in her left hand. I notice that their free hands are enfolded next to each other. I put it out of my mind. I take another sip, close my eyes, and think of all the beauty that surrounds me.

There is soft whispering next to me. And soon I can hear the sound of sleeping bags unzipping. I hear the shuffle of the bedding and clothing. And as I hear the soft moans from the bodies next to me, I can almost feel the fingers and tongues and lips exploring. I turn my body to the side, away from the struggle, close my eyes, and wish for sleep.

"Hope we didn't bother you last night," says Mary as she picks up her coffee cup.

"No," I say. "Not at all." I lie a little.

"You know, if you want to join in ..." Mary's voice trails.

I shake my head. "No, thank you," I say. "It's just not my style."

"Understand," says Mary. "But if you change your mind, we're kind of free spirits, and sometimes you just gotta do what you gotta do."

I nod and think back to knee-walking across the tent floor and touching Billy.

"Let me rephrase that," says Mary. "Sometime you just gotta do what you *want* to do."

We go into the town of Waterton to get some supplies. We need more food. Not freeze-dried, but real food. And more wine. Definitely more wine. Both Mary and Jane go for Chardonnay, just my style. We stop at an equipment supply store for a tent. The store is out of tents. I tell them to be cool. They can stay with me for another day, although I am thinking maybe two. I like these girls. They are free spirits. Do what they want to do. I could learn something from them.

Chloe

While we are in town, we stop at Zum's Eatery. I've had enough freeze-dried, and we all would like a nice, hot breakfast. The food is good and plentiful. While we are seated at a window table, I look out the window and see a moose just sauntering down the street. Some people stop to look, but others, obviously locals, just go about their business. We look at a map from the outfit store and decide on a hiking trip for the day. There is a hiking trail that starts at the town of Waterton. We drive to the town campsite and park the car. The trails start right from town, which is perfect. We can leave our car here for now and take a hike, as they say.

The Bertha Lake Trail is a trail that will take us from Lower Bertha Falls to Upper Bertha Falls. The map says it's 5.2 kilometers, or a little over three miles. We can do that. We tell the waitress our plans, and she says if we are going all the way, we will need a permission slip, as the trail will be right along the border with the United States. I did not realize that we were that close. But we go back to the store and get a permission slip to take with us.

We drive the car to the start of the trail and start out, leaving the cooler in the trunk. If the ice melts, we can just go back and get some more. It's much better than driving to the campsite, dropping things off, and coming back. There is a sign that says the trail is open from July 1 to August 31. Not a long season, but this is Canada, and these are the Rocky Mountains. Don't wanna get anyone lost in a blizzard in June.

There is a slight grade that, at this altitude, takes a

little longer. After about a mile or so, the trail branches to the left. We take the trail and get a beautiful view of Upper Waterton Lake and a mountain, which I take to be Mount Richards from the map. Later, we stop at a beautiful waterfall.

At the bottom of the falls is Bertha Creek. The rocks are laid out like large logs or stony cathedral steps with water flowing over them, only to be captured and cascade again down the slope. We continue our trek and see Upper Waterton Lake and Upper Bertha Falls.

We have been going longer than we thought. We thought it would only take a couple of hours, but the altitude and grade slow us down. When we reach the end of the trail, it is five hours past breakfast. It is time to have lunch. No time to make it back to the camp, but plenty of time to make it to Zum's Eatery.

I've seen two beautiful lakes here: Lower and Upper Waterton. And they are beautiful, for sure. We're in the Rocky Mountains, for gosh sakes. But I've seen a lot of beautiful lakes. I've been to Glacier Park, Banff, Lake Moraine, Lake Louise, Emerald Lake. And although the lakes and mountains here are beautiful, to be sure, what really struck me were the waterfalls, Lower and Upper Bertha. I've seen a lot of waterfalls, but with most of them, the water comes straight down, some almost in a column. Although the stream that feeds these falls is only a few feet across, it spills onto a horizontal basalt rock formation, almost stair-like. As the water falls onto the first horizontal column, it spreads out a bit. Then it falls onto the next rock column and spreads out again and in turn, cascades over to the next column. And with each extrusion, the water bubbles white, so that when it finally reaches the downstream, there is an inverted V of white phosphorescence, giving proof to its name, Bridal Veil Falls. It is truly one of the most beautiful sights in nature.

Another night with a nice campfire. Another night of conversation. Another night of feeling the ache of the thousand steps of a nature hike. Lying in my sleeping bag, I think of Mary's words: "Sometimes you just gotta do what you *want* to do." I've always been straight, ever since I found out about these things. And I still am. Can't change what I am, and I wouldn't want to. But I wonder what it would be like to be with the one who knows you like you know yourself, where your zones are, what to touch and how to touch and what to do. And I think back to the rodeo, with Stacy riding her horse bareback and the crowds cheering and the beer spilling as I pump my fist into the air. And the speaker blasting out the words "Live like you were dyin'." And I feel a warmth growing in my body. And I roll over and try to go to sleep.

Another day in the mountains. Mary and Jane want to go on another hike. They ask me if I want to go. I tell them my feet are tired from yesterday's hike. They take some food and head out, saying they are going to hike to Crandell Lake and they should be back for supper.

I'm glad they are having a good time. And I am glad I have some more time to myself. I enjoy their company immensely, but I need some time to veg. It's still a little windy up here, so I park myself on the leeward side of Big Blue and open a book.

We are at the campfire. Mary and Jane are engaged in conversation. The fire is hot and feels good against the cool night air. They are sitting across from me, sharing a log. For each of them, separate hands hold a glass of Chardonnay, and the common hands are enfolded together. They stop talking for a moment and turn their attention to me. They seem so at ease. So sure of themselves. Mary's mouth is moving. I can't make it out. She is not talking, just moving her lips, like she is whispering to me. It was a simple sentence. Although I cannot hear the words, I know what they are. They are the words I heard myself repeating. I meet her gaze for a moment and then turn to the fire, the fire that is warming me on this cool summer's night.

Chapter 26

"Cup of coffee?" Jane asks.

"Yeah, that would be nice," I say.

Jane pours a cup and hands it to me.

I blow softly across the top of the cup as the steam drifts over the rim in the cool morning air.

"Did we bother you last night?" she asks.

I shake my head. "No," I say.

Jane puts her forefinger to my lips. "Don't worry," she says. "We all start out that way." She brings her finger down. "We all start out with other people telling us how we should think and how we should act. It isn't until later that we develop the courage to think for ourselves."

"But I'm straight," I say.

Jane throws back her hair. "That's fine," she says. "You can be straight and still do what you want to do. No guilt. No regrets."

"I appreciate that," I say.

Jane gives me a hug, and I hug her back. "I think I'm going home now," I say. I didn't mean to say those words. I didn't even think about them. Those words just tumbled out of my mouth. They came without thought, without consideration. And after the words were out there and lying on the table in plain sight, it felt good. It felt right. It's time to go home.

Chloe

It's morning, and I have my gear and sleeping bag in the car. Big Blue is still up. Mary and Jane are standing in front of me.

"You need help with the tent?" asks Mary.

I shake my head.

"Could you give us a lift into town?" asks Jane. "Maybe we can scrounge up a tent."

I look at these two people I have just met, and yet I feel like I have known them for a long time. I look at Big Blue. Even with the guy ropes taut, the roof ruffles with the wind. It's almost like Big Blue is fighting, straining, showing it can stand the wind, begging me to let it stay … stay in the mountains.

I smile and turn to the girls. "Why don't you two take the tent?" I say, more than ask.

"Your tent?" Mary exclaims. "You want us to take your tent?"

"I think Big Blue would like it here in the mountains," I say.

"What about you?" asks Jane.

"Me," I say. "I'm headed for clean sheets and fluffy pillows. I'm going home, and eastern Montana and North Dakota are flat and dry and windy. There are plenty of motels along the way. And when I get home, I don't think I'll be back for a while. Big Blue deserves better."

"Well," says Mary. "That's very generous of you."

"Well, you taught me something," I say.

"You mean we taught you how to do the things we do?" asks Jane. "Like last night?"

I shake my head. "No," I say. "Not that. You taught me to be myself and not be afraid of the choices that I make."

I take one last look at Big Blue. I hate saying goodbye to Big Blue. But Big Blue doesn't deserve gathering dust in the bottom of a closet for thirty years. Big Blue should be in the mountains, with Mary and Jane. And with Billy. I turn back to my erstwhile comrades. I give them both a hug, hop in the car, and head for home.

In the middle of Montana, near Billings, the eastbound interstate diverges. Interstate 94, the northern route, takes you to the spectacular Badlands of North Dakota and Medora, where Teddy Roosevelt went to search for answers and found himself. On the eastern edge of North Dakota are the cities of Fargo and Moorehead, Minnesota, separated by the Red River. The land there is some of the flattest habitable land on the planet. And the soil is some of the richest. It is the bottom of Lake Agassiz, a remnant of the Ice Age, where ice covered much of North America. When the ice melted, Lake Agassiz was formed. As the fish in the lake died over centuries, the decayed flesh lay at the bottom of the lake. When the lake receded, its dried lake bottom was one of the most fertile valleys on the continent. The major cash crop in the Red River Valley today is sugar beets.

The southern divergent is Interstate 90, the road I took west. Going back, I could revisit this and the Black Hills and the South Dakota Badlands. But I did not decide to go back the way I came to revisit those areas. No, I am taking the southern route to revisit a place in northeastern Wyoming called Devils Tower. I feel I have some unfinished business there.

I turn off the interstate at Highway 14, the road to Devils Tower. As I drive along, I see the prairie dogs pop in and out of their holes. And as Devils Tower comes in sight, it seems that the prairie dogs welcome me back. They are like a wave, popping into their holes on a line perpendicular to my pathway, only to reemerge as I pass by and, by this inertia, push me forward. It is if they are welcoming me back, in the same way as they had sent me out into the wilderness. And I smile.

I arrive at dusk. There are no other cars and no other people around. I get out of my car and walk across sandy soil and around some bushes and tumbleweeds. I am standing before this great monolith. It was from here that I really left on my journey. I feel a tingling around me. Now I know why the native peoples of this land come to this place to be with the spirits in the ground. Fireflies flit around me. As they grow in number, one brushes against my left arm. Another hits my leg, but softly. I know it's my imagination, but they seem to be rising from the ground. There is a glow in the twilight as the fireflies increase in number, and soon, the glow illuminates the area around me. I lift my head to this grand monolith. I close my eyes. My whole body tingles. It is as if the spirits are ascending from the ground and are huddling around me. I can feel them touching my skin with soft caresses. I spread my arms from my sides and open my palms in acceptance. I open my mouth and shout at the top of my voice, *"I am Chloe. I am alive. And I am here!"*

I am lying in a bed with clean sheets (I hope) and fluffy pillows (not so much). I made it to a motel in Spearfish, South Dakota. I was lucky to get a room.

This is a popular place in the summer. Sturgis is right down the road. Every year, there is a motorcycle rally that brings in gobs of people. And the crowd spills over into the surrounding area. At the desk, they told me that I got the last room. Happy for that. I really don't want another night sleeping in my car. I took a chance going back to Devils Tower, but it was worth it. It seemed like it was the beginning and the culmination of my journey. I have never been very religious. But who can quantitatively say, with assurance, that there are no spirits in the ground? We have only five senses. What if we were given a sixth or seventh sense? We would be like a mole that is blind, suddenly given sight. What wonders of the universe would be there to be discovered! Who can claim to know all the knowledge in the universe? All I know is that I stood before a monolith in the dark and was illuminated by a swarm of fireflies that appeared to be rising from the ground.

Chapter 27

I'VE HAD ANOTHER SHUDDER. IT IS LIKE A MINISEIZURE. IT takes my whole body and freezes it for just a second, and then it is gone. I am awake in my bed and wondering what is happening to me. They may be seizures, but I am calling them shudders for now. This is the fourth shudder I've had on this trip. I don't know what it is, but something is happening. I'm going to call my doctor and get a complete physical. And I'm going to call that clinic—the clinic where I was conceived.

As I drive eastward on Interstate 90, I am passing the turnoff to the Wounded Knee massacre site. I was there on my way out, and the experience has never left me. I wonder if Billy Two Bears has been there. And I wonder what he would do if he could go back in time to that day on December 29, 1890. A day where a half white, half Native American could stand on a hill and watch as the United States Army surrounded the huddled Lakota in the snow. What would he do when the Hotchkiss cannons hurled their shards of metal toward the flesh below? Would he realize that these were his people killing his people? And what would he do if he revisited the battleground on the next day? Would he trudge through the snow, being careful not to trip over the bodies strewn about? And when he came to the body of Chief Spotted Elk, a frozen arm reaching skyward and lifeless eyes pointing to some distant focus, would he drop to his knees in the snow and pound his fist into the frozen ground? Would his tears, as they left his cheek, freeze before they reached the ground?

I know that hitchhiking is illegal on interstate highways. But as I pass each entrance ramp, I glance to the right, maybe to catch the sight of a young man in shorts and a T-shirt with his thumb out. And maybe he will have a hat with his hair piled up beneath it. Or maybe the back hair will just flow freely to his shoulders. Yes, I look for Billy Two Bears as I drive. And if I see him, I'm going to have a talk with that bad boy.

I'm home at last. The house is somewhat barren. My half sister, Lisa, is in charge of my father's estate. She has cleaned the house of the nonessentials. There is no living room furniture, no dining room furniture. Everything is out of the basement. Lisa will let me stay here for a while until I get situated. So I just have the bare essentials: my bedroom, bathroom, and dinette table for breakfast and lunch. It's probably time for me to move on anyway. Sell the house, settle the estate, move on. I'll look for an apartment soon, but tonight, I am just glad to be home in my own bed, safe and sound.

I was lucky to get in to see my doctor, Dr. Stevenson, so quickly. When the nurse asked me my symptoms, I think she moved some things around to get me in quickly. So I am at the clinic in the waiting room. I've read the newspaper this morning and am not interested in the magazines on the table in front of me. But I have my Sudoku to keep me busy for a while. It has five stars, so it should be interesting.

I'm almost done with my puzzle when the nurse comes out and escorts me to a room. I sit on a chair and resume my puzzle as the nurse takes my pulse and blood pressure. She makes some notes on the computer and tells me the good doctor will be with me soon; then she is up and out the door. I no more than put my pen to the paper when there is a knock on the door. I wonder why doctors always knock on the door while the patient is waiting. What do they think we are doing?

The door opens without me acknowledging the knock. Dr. Stevenson comes in and offers his hand. I stand and shake his hand and sit down again. The good doctor sits at the minidesk beside me, his hands on his lap, ignoring the computer beside him.

"Well," he says. "What brings you in here this time?"

I take a deep breath. "Thank you for seeing me so soon," I start.

He nods his head but says nothing.

"I … I've had these, ah, I don't know what to call them," I say. "They are like little seizures."

"Seizures?" Dr. Stevenson repeats, squinting his eyes.

"Well," I say, "I don't know what seizures are, but it is like my whole body just freezes up for a second. It is just for a very short time—I would say a second or two—and then they are gone. They are more like shudders. It's like my whole body shudders, but just for a moment, and then it is gone."

Dr. Stevenson nods. "Is there any pain?" he asks.

I shake my head. "No, there is no pain, just … ah … shudders," I say.

Dr. Stevenson massages his jaw with his right thumb

and forefinger. "Humm," he says. "Just a shudder and no pain," he says to no one. "And just for a second or two."

"Yeah, I guess," I say. "I'm sure it's nothing, but—"

"No. You were right to come in here." He turns to his computer and pushes some keys. "We're going to have to give you some tests. I'm checking here ..."

Then he turns to me and asks, "Are you busy next Thursday?"

I often think, as I lie here in my bed, about my relationship with my mother. I call her that because I don't know what else to call her. I was told that she died in childbirth, giving birth to me. And I never did the math. There was no need to. Can I call it a lie? Is it a lie when someone is trying to protect you? I know my father was trying to protect me by not telling me until he had to. Until he ran out of time. But I'm glad he told me. At least, I think I'm glad. Would I act differently if I had never known? Of course I would. But it's better to know. But what do I know? I know that I am a copy, an exact copy of my mother, Jenny. But do I have a soul? Is there enough soul for both of us, or did she take it with her? And how long will I live? Can I have children too? Will it hurt me if I do? I would like to have children someday, I suppose. I haven't given it much thought. I've got other things to worry about now. *Let's take it one step at a time. Let's wait to see what the good doctor has to say.*

I answer the phone. It is Dr. Stevenson. He wants me to come in to see him. He says he would normally put my results on my portal. But there is something he wants to talk to me about. It's best if I come in and go over the results in person.

"Have a seat," says Dr. Stevenson, pointing to a chair in the examining room.

I move to the chair and sit. "So, what's up, Doc?" I say.

Dr. Stevenson smiles. I'm sure he's heard that a thousand times, but I just couldn't resist. Need to break the tension.

"So, Chloe," says Dr. Stevenson. "Because of your symptoms, we've done a pretty thorough examination."

I nod and look down at his chart.

"The EEG came back normal," Dr. Stevenson says. "And the brain scan came back normal as well. As you know, we even did an EKG. Normal." He looks down at the clipboard in his hands. "I really wanted to be thorough because of your symptoms. So I ran a couple of extra tests." He raises his head and looks directly at me.

"Chloe," he says. "Did you know that you are pregnant?"

"Thank you for seeing me so soon, Doctor," I say.

Dr. Ahmann nods. "When I got your call, I was glad to hear from you."

"Yes, thank you," I say. "Could we—"

"Yes. Let's go into my office."

He turns and heads down the hallway. I follow. He opens the door and holds it for me as I walk into his office. He motions for a chair, and I sit. He sits down in his desk chair. "It's good to see you again, Chloe," he says. "I was wondering how you were doing." He takes a long look at me. "So how are you doing?"

I look up at the wall and see the plaques and awards. I turn back to him. "Tell me about Dolly," I say.

His eyes go down to the floor. "Ah yes. Dolly."

"Yes, tell me about her," I say. "Tell me how she lived." I pause for a moment. "And how she died."

"Well," says Dr. Ahmann. "I told you the particulars about her death before. And we don't really know why she died so young. I can only speculate. She was a real sheep, a healthy sheep. But since she was a clone, there may be something that was different, even though the chromosomes were exact duplicates. Maybe there is something like, like, ah, I call it a shaving off. Just a little of something, call it sheepdom or sheepness if you will, was shaved off. She was a live sheep, but there was something different, maybe something missing." He raises his eyes to me. I can't tell if his expression is one of pleading or apologizing. "Do you get what I mean?" he says.

"I get the picture," I say. "But something is happening to me that no one can explain. I've been to my doctor and had tests, but no one can explain what it is."

Dr. Ahmann raises his eyes to me. "Tell me," he says.

"I get, ah, what I call shudders," I say. "They are like mini-seizures. They only last for a second or so. They do not hurt, and they don't have a lasting effect on me."

Dr. Ahmann puts his head down, and his left hand comes up to cradle it. He massages his forehead with his fingers. He does not say a word, but I know that something is wrong.

"What?" I ask, only more of a demand.

Still massaging his forehead and without looking up, he says, "That's the symptom that Dolly had."

There is a long pause. Neither of us speaks for two minutes, by the clock.

"Doctor," I manage meekly. "What are my chances?"

Dr. Ahmann takes a deep breath and raises his eyes to meet my anxious gaze. "I don't know," he says. "You're the first and only one, as far as I know. Maybe you're stronger than Dolly. Dolly died of lung cancer. But maybe she got an infection that lowered her resistance and she couldn't fight the cancer. Maybe if she had not had an infection, she could have fought the cancer and lived longer. We just don't know. The best advice I can give you is to stay healthy and not to strain yourself. Your body has only so much energy. If you take care of yourself, I see no reason that you could not live to have a long, healthy life."

After a pause, I ask, "Do I have a soul?"

There is a half laugh from him. "Of course you have a soul. Don't be ridiculous. Everyone has a soul. You are unique. Yes, I believe you have a soul."

"I am not unique," I say. "I am a copy."

"Yes," he says. "But you are a unique copy. You have a soul."

There is a long pause. I'm wondering where I should go next. Then it blurts out of my mouth. "Doctor," I say. "I'm pregnant."

"My god," he says. "That does complicate matters."

"Yes, it does," I say with almost a laugh.

Dr. Ahmann takes a deep breath and lets it out slowly. Once again, his hand is massaging his chin. He leans back in his chair and swivels a bit. His hands go to his lap as the chair comes to a stop. "You know that takes a lot of energy from your body," he says.

"Yeah, I know that," I respond.

"And I'm not recommending ..." he says and pauses. "But there are alternatives."

I close my eyes and nod. "I know," I say. "But I don't know who else to turn to. What do you recommend? As a doctor, I mean."

"I can't make that kind of decision for you," he says. "You are a healthy, vibrant woman now. But the way I see it is … you can live a long life, or you can have a baby. But you can't have both."

As I drive home, the words ring in my ears and into my soul. "You can live a long life, or you can have a baby, but you can't have both." My god, I'm lucky if I don't drive off the road. What is this thing growing inside of me? It's just a zygote, a minimass of tissue, without any real form. A simple procedure and it can be swiftly swept away. I know where the clinic is. It's almost on my way home. I could make a quick turn, and it could be done. I know it's not that easy. It takes time. It should take time. This is not a spur-of-the-moment decision. I wonder how long it took for my father to make his decision, to start me from a dish. What would my father want me to do? Jeez, I wish I could talk to him. Ask him what I should do. I would trust his advice. But he is gone. And I don't have anyone that I could talk to.

I'm crying. I can't help it. It is too overwhelming. I'm in my house, in my bedroom, lying on my bed. Let the dam burst. Let it flow. Let's get this over with.

The doorbell rings. I ain't answering it. It rings again. No way. I bury my head in my pillow. I hear the lock on the front door click. My head is off the pillow. I hear the door open and, "Chloe, are you home?" echoes through the semiempty house. I rise from the bed and wipe my eyes with the edge of the sheet.

"I'm up here," I yell.

"Okay." It's my half sister Lisa's voice. "Just came to pick up some things."

I walk down the half stairs to meet her.

Lisa looks at me. "You been cryin'?" she asks.

"Nah," I manage.

Lisa cants her head so she can get a better look at my eyes. "Chloe?" she asks questioningly, like she knows something is wrong.

I know my eyes are red and there are probably some tearstains on my cheeks that the sheet missed. I manage a half smile and wipe my cheeks with the back of my hands.

"What's wrong?" Lisa asks again.

I shrug. "Nothing," I say.

Lisa gives me that "you don't fool me" look. "Boy problems?" she asks.

I nod.

"Joe?"

I nod my head. If it would only be that simple. "I broke up with Joe," I say.

"Well, that explains it," she says.

An easy out. "Yeah," I correct myself.

"Well," says Lisa. "I just came over to get some more of Dad's things. Anything I can get for you?"

I shake my head.

"Wanna talk about it?" she asks. "It's good to have an ear."

"I know," I say. "Thanks, but I'll be okay."

Lisa has collected some things and left. I don't know what I will do. Why does the decision have to be up to me? Why can't I just be in a car accident, be thrown against the steering wheel, and have a miscarriage? It would be done. It would not have to be my decision. I pound my forehead against the door. Why (pound) does it (pound) have to (pound) be me (pound)?

It's time to get my things in order. I look around my bedroom. The sheets are half off the bed. I have socks and underwear strewn across the floor. And my backpack is sitting against the wall, leaning back as if it knows something. Real cocky. I walk over to it and give it a kick. My toes land softly, telling me that I haven't even emptied my backpack from the trip. God, I'm a mess.

Okay, let's start. Let's clean up this mess. I pick up my privates from the floor and fling them into my laundry basket, half hidden in the closet. Even though I will be going to bed soon, I make the bed—well, sort of. I walk over to my backpack and apologize to it. I am down on my knees unzipping the zippers and unflapping the flaps and unpocketing the pockets. Socks, underwear, T-shirts, and sweaters are on the floor next to the backpack. I am sure everything is out, but one last look. I lift the backpack up, invert it, and give it a good shake. As the flaps flop down, a paper clip and a stick of spearmint gum topple to the floor. Another shake, and a white feather appears from the large pocket and drifts slowly to the carpet. My arms quiver as the backpack loosens from my grip and clanks to the floor beside me. I stare at Billy's eagle feather. A calmness comes over me as I pick it up and remember the words that Billy said.

There are times when something just hits you in the face. Through happenstance or by design, the universe takes a turn, and what was once an impossibility is now possible. An unsolvable puzzle is now solved. They could be lying in the bottom of a nest, or just floating from the sky to the ground. There must be a thousand-million-billion white feathers in this world. But this one was meant for me. It is something that Billy wanted me to find. And to find it at the absolute right time. He knew. He is talking to me now. And I know what to tell him. But I don't have to tell him. He already knows.

"Thank you for seeing me on such short notice," I say.

Dr. Ahmann nods. "It's good to see you too," he says. "Let's go into my office."

I sit down. "You told me that I could have a baby or have a long life but I can't have both."

"It's not an exact science, but that's what I believe, based on the information that I have."

"Well, I've decided to have the baby."

"You know the odds."

"I've learned a lot about myself in the last few months. And I've lived a lot as well. I was given life—maybe it was a mistake, but I was given it nonetheless. And I am here. I feel like I have lived a full life."

"But you are only twenty-one. You've got a lot of living to do."

"You told me once that there is a theory that Dolly was born at an advanced age, the age of her mother or donor."

"That may or may not be true. It's only a theory based on the autopsy. Dolly's organs appeared older than her chronological age."

"Well, if it is true, and you add my mother's age at her death to my age, I'd say I have lived a long life."

"It's just a theory, Chloe."

"But it's a theory I can live with. Or should I say I can die with. I'm very comfortable with whatever happens. I have been given life, and now I have a chance to give life.

Maybe that will make me a complete woman, a complete human, instead of a shadow of someone else. I can be myself and give of myself, by myself. My father made a decision to bring me into the world. Now I am making the decision to bring someone else into the world. This is where I belong. This is why I am here."

I'm standing before a full-length mirror. An ashen face stares back at me. The hair is flat against her head, and pale arms hang loose against her body. The maternity smock is pink floral. The hands go to her distended belly as a contraction starts. There is a grimace on her face for a moment, which turns to a dull smile with the release of the contraction.

There is the sound of a car in the driveway, a slammed car door, footfalls to the front door, and doorbell chimes. The door opens, and Lisa walks in.

"Ready to go?" asks Lisa in loud voice.

I turn from the lady in the mirror with the ashen face. I pinch my cheeks and feel a blush. "Yes," I say. "I'm ready."

Chapter 28

SPRING HAS COME EARLY THIS YEAR, AND I HAVE THE CAR window rolled down. I want to feel the wind against my face and toss what's left of my matted hair. I want to feel nature on my skin. How much time do I have left? I smile and mouth the words "A lifetime."

Lisa turns from the windshield and looks at me. "What?" she asks.

"It's so nice of you to help me, to take me to the hospital," I say.

"You're my sister," says Lisa.

"I'm not," I say.

"Well, okay," says Lisa. "My half sister, then."

I shake my head. "No, Lisa."

Lisa looks at me. "Chloe," she says. "I know."

I look at her.

Lisa nods. "When my father—ah, our father—became ill," she says, "he called me in to talk to me. He told me everything. He wanted me to know about you in case something happened. And he told me about Dr. Ahmann. And I have talked to him. I know you are your mother. You may call me your half sister, or whatever, but I consider you my true sister. In our minds, we share the same father. In my mind, you are my true sister, and that is all that counts. I am very proud of the decision that you have made. I know it was a very difficult decision.

But if something does happen to you, please know that I will take your daughter and raise her as my own. She is family. And that is all that matters."

"But at your age ..." I say.

"Ah, it will be fun," she says. "It will be like a second childhood for me."

I feel my eyes start to water. "Thank you, Lisa," I say. "Thank you for being here for me."

Lisa smiles. "You're family," she says.

We stop at a stoplight. We are getting near to the hospital.

"Did you ever consider an alternative?" Lisa asks, turning to me.

"What, you mean an abortion?" I say.

"Well, yeah," she says. "I mean, just ..."

I nod. "Yeah," I say. "I considered it. At the beginning. When it would have been easy." I put my hand on my distended belly and feel a tiny foot migrate across my abdomen. "But I remembered what someone told me, what seems like a long time ago. He said, 'A man looks at something and sees what it is. A wise man sees what it can become.'"

As I feel the fading start, I look up at my sister, Lisa.

"What shall we call her?" Lisa asks.

"Jenny," I say.

"Yes," says Lisa. "After your mother."

"No," I say. "After me."

As the fading proceeded, Chloe looked down at her daughter suckling at her breast. Tears welled in her eyes. "Take good care of my daughter," she said. She closed her eyes as the tears overflowed the lids and trickled down her cheeks. She felt her arms grow slack as the light faded from her eyes.

If she had been alive, she would have heard the monitor switch from counting beeps to a high-pitched drone. If she had been alive, she would have felt her sister, Lisa, gently pick up her daughter and place her in her arms. And she would have heard Lisa say, through tears, the only word Chloe had longed to hear: "Jenny."

The End

Printed and bound by PG in the USA